She frowned.

'How old are you?' this, she couldn't say, except to acknowledge that something didn't gel about this man. Most of her brother's lame ducks were academics. Most of them were earnest, scholarly, modest and so wrapped up in their chosen fields, she occasionally got the feeling she could dance naked on the dining table and not even be noticed.

Richard Moore, she mused, might be an impoverished photographer but she had the strong feeling he didn't fit into any of the other categories.

Lindsay Armstrong was born in South Africa but now lives in Australia with her New Zealand-born husband and their five children. They have lived in nearly every state of Australia and tried their hand at some unusual, for them, occupations, such as farming and horse training—all grist to the mill for a writer! Lindsay started writing romances when their youngest child began school and she was left feeling at a loose end. She is still doing it and loving it.

Recent titles by the same author:

WILDCAT WIFE

IN BED WITH
A STRANGER

BY
LINDSAY ARMSTRONG

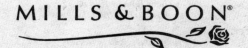

MILLS & BOON®

*All the characters in this book have no existence outside the imagination
of the author, and have no relation whatsoever to anyone bearing the
same name or names. They are not even distantly inspired by any
individual known or unknown to the author, and all the incidents are
pure invention.*

*First published in Great Britain 1998
Harlequin Mills & Boon Limited,
Eton House, 18-24 Paradise Road, Richmond, Surrey TW9 1SR*

© Lindsay Armstrong 1998

ISBN 0 263 81042 9

*Set in Times Roman 10½ on 12 pt.
01-9807-47764 C1*

*Printed and bound in Norway
by AiT Trondheim AS, Trondheim*

CHAPTER ONE

LOUISE BROWN had just stepped out of the shower when the doorbell rang. She grabbed a towel, dried herself cursorily and struggled into a cotton wrapper.

It rang again as she ran downstairs, a longer ring this time, followed by a cheeky little tiddly pom tattoo. She muttered beneath her breath, tripped on the last step and finally opened the door, breathing raggedly. 'Yes!'

'Ah,' the tall stranger on the doorstep said, looking her over comprehensively. 'Who are you?'

She stared bemusedly at the man. He was big with broad, powerful shoulders, lean hips, and he was at least six feet four. She blinked twice and noted that he was casually dressed in jeans, a khaki shirt and dusty boots, then she shook her head as if to clear her mind and said rather wryly, 'If you don't know, what are you doing ringing my bell? May I ask who *you* are?'

He had very blue eyes, she saw in the slight pause that followed. She noted that he allowed them to drift over her again, this time with a wicked little glint of appreciation, before he said, 'Richard Moore, ma'am. How do you do? I've come to stay. Did—?'

'Oh, no, you have not,' she gasped, having glanced down to see that her thin cotton wrapper had moulded itself to her damp body like a second skin.

'I can assure you—' He paused to look at the number on the door and down at the piece of paper in his hand. 'This is the Brown residence, is it not?'

'Yes, but—'

'Then I'm at the right place. So—' he looked at her with a tinge of impatience '—if you wouldn't mind letting me in, we could sort it out more comfortably.'

Louise drew herself up to her full five feet eight. 'There is nothing to sort out. This is my house! Would you go way, please?' She started to close the door.

But Richard Moore put a foot in it and said with distinct irritation, 'Now look here, lady, it would appear that Neil forgot to tell you about me. He certainly forgot to mention to *me* that he had a mistress in residence, but—'

'Neil!' Louise cried. 'Oh, for crying out loud! Why does he keep doing this to me? I suppose you're one of his lame ducks. But for your information, Mr Moore, I am his *sister*, not his mistress.'

Richard Moore blinked and tried not to laugh—unsuccessfully. Finally, sobering, he said gravely, 'My most abject apologies, Miss Brown. It is Miss Brown, I take it?'

'Yes. So?' Louise returned dangerously.

'Nothing. I wondered whether I might be addressing his married sister, that's all,' Richard Moore said hastily. 'Uh—but the fact of the matter, Miss Brown, is that Neil invited me to stay for a fortnight.'

'That's impossible!' Louise objected. 'I have no intention of sharing my home with a complete stranger for a fortnight.'

'If I could just have a word with him—'

'That's also impossible. He's in the wilds of East Gippsland and he not only forgot *you*, Mr Moore, he forgot to take his mobile phone. Typical Neil,' she said bitterly.

Richard Moore folded his arms and regarded her steadily. 'So what do you suggest I do, Miss Brown?'

'What do you mean?'

'Wander the streets?'

'Well—' Louise hesitated '—there is a dazzling array of accommodation to choose from on the Coast. Oh, look, come in,' she said frustratedly. 'I'll ring around for you.' She swung the door open. 'Just wait in there, please, while I put some clothes on.' She gestured imperiously towards the lounge.

Richard Moore picked up his two bags and followed her directions. He turned to watch as she retreated up the stairs, then he raised an eyebrow and wondered why Neil had omitted to mention his stunning sister. Had she realized how little the damp cotton robe had concealed her beautiful figure? He smiled faintly at the memory of it, luscious and full in all the right places, exquisitely slim about the waist, long legs...

Then there was all that damp hair that would dry to ash-blonde, he guessed, lovely smooth skin, green eyes with little gold flecks in them, a slightly square jaw and a pair of lips that were coolly moulded to a severe kind of perfection that simply invited thoughts of rendering them soft and crushed...

He grimaced and shrugged—and remembered that Neil Brown was as absent-minded as he was clever, at times an endearing trait, at others extremely frustrating. Such as right now, for example. What the hell was he doing in East Gippsland when he should be here?

And what the hell am I going to do for the next fortnight? he pondered. Foist myself on his gorgeous but definitely unwelcoming sister? He stared across the room unseeingly, then that wicked glint came to his blue eyes again as he remembered her term—'lame ducks'.

In the meantime, Louise was regarding herself exasperatedly in her bedroom mirror. She'd only been caught having a shower that late in the morning because she'd just come in from having a swim in the sea. And she might as well have answered the door with no clothes on at all—something that obviously hadn't escaped Richard Moore. Why hadn't she taken her time and got dressed properly? He might even have gone away, she thought angrily.

Then she sighed and started to change. What on earth was she going to do with him? Where had Neil found him and what had he planned to do with him for a whole fortnight?

All this brought a clear picture of her brother Neil to her mind. A zoologist and impassioned conservationist, Neil could infuriate her like no other with his absent-minded ways. Then again, she reminded herself, she also loved him dearly, not only as a brother but as a wise and warm humanitarian.

They owned this town house at MacRae Place jointly and for the most part it was a comfortable arrangement. Neil didn't spend a lot of time at home so when he did, usually with someone to stay who was as passionate about conservation or zoology as he was, Louise made the necessary adjustments. She always kept the spare bedroom made up and the freezer well stocked because a lot of these visitations did come out of the blue. This was different, though, she thought. Or, put it this way, this *man* was different.

She stopped and frowned as something seemed to

hover on the edge of her mind; but it refused to reveal itself and she concentrated on getting dressed, and on ways and means of dealing with Mr Richard Moore and his all-seeing blue eyes.

'There you are,' she said, coming down the stairs about twenty minutes later. She'd put on grey shorts, a short-sleeved primrose silk blouse and a pair of grey kid flat shoes. Her long hair was pulled back into a single thick plait and she'd applied a minimum of make-up.

'Still here, yes,' Richard murmured, standing up politely. 'It's a very nice place you have.'

'Thanks.' Louise glanced around the lounge with pride. It was a light, spacious room with pale apricot walls and white wooden louvres at the windows. There were built-in bookcases that held not only books but an interesting collection of bric-à-brac. Three comfortable settees covered in sage-green suede were grouped around a vast low coffee table. Paintings and prints hung on the walls and an upright piano stood in one corner. It was a lived-in and relaxing room with individual charm.

'So tell me about yourself, Mr Moore,' she invited, turning back to him coolly. 'How did you meet Neil?' She sat down.

After a moment he sat opposite her. 'Photographing rhinos at the Western Plains Zoo, Dubbo.'

Louise grimaced.

Richard raised an eyebrow. 'You disapprove?'

'Hardly. It's just that since they started that breeding programme at Dubbo Neil has been not only besotted but verging on paranoid.'

'They are an extremely endangered species,' Richard commented.

Louise glanced at him through her lashes. 'I do know that. So you're a photographer? Is that all you do?'

'Uh—well, yes.'

She eyed him. He was sitting forward with his hands clasped between his knees. His fair hair was straight, longish, roughly cut and prone to falling in his eyes. There were blue shadows on his jaw—he obviously hadn't shaved—and his khaki shirt had several patches on it. His dusty boots were scuffed.

Yet none of this, not even a certain weariness about his eyes, diminished the impact of a confident and fine physical specimen who was good-looking as well.

She came out of her reverie, aware suddenly that those blue eyes were becoming amused and quizzical. 'I see. I suppose that's why Neil has taken you under his wing?'

Richard Moore blinked, but as Louise rather pointedly examined his dusty attire and scuffed boots he said slowly, 'It can be a hard field to break into.'

She frowned. 'How old are you?' What compelled her to ask this, she couldn't quite say, except to acknowledge that something didn't gel about this man. Most of Neil's lame ducks were academics. Most of them were earnest, scholarly, modest and so wrapped up in their chosen fields, she occasionally got the feeling she could dance naked on the dining table and not even be noticed. Most of them were distinctly dysfunctional when it came to socializing, and especially so with women.

Richard Moore, she mused, might be an impoverished photographer but she had the strong feeling he didn't fit into any of the other categories. There also lurked behind those blue eyes a sort of arrogance that didn't deal kindly with fools.

'I'm thirty-two,' he said, and raised an eyebrow at her.

'Isn't that—sorry—but isn't that a little late to be trying to break into a career?' she asked slowly, ignoring
the query in his eyes.

He paused. 'Uh...well, with Neil's help, who knows
what might come my way?'

Louise opened her mouth, then had another idea.
'Would you mind waiting a moment?' she asked, standing up smoothly.

'Not at all.' He watched her as she started to walk out
of the room, watched the way the light grey fabric of
her shorts moulded her thighs with each fluid stride and
how the primrose blouse rose and fell over her breasts
at the same time. Their gazes locked just before she
moved past him and she couldn't miss the sheer appreciation of her figure again in his eyes; but she only tilted
her chin and swept on.

She went straight to her brother's study, fuming
slightly, only to close her eyes exasperatedly because
finding anything was going to be like finding a needle
in a haystack.

'You may be a brilliant zoologist, dear brother mine,'
she muttered crossly, 'but you are also the most disor-
ganized person I know! How could we be so different?'
Then she swore beneath her breath as she accidentally
dislodged a stack of folders on the desk and they showered their contents to the floor. But it wasn't a total disaster because the object revealed beneath them turned
out to be Neil's diary.

She pounced on it, flipped through the pages and there
under today's date was the entry: *Richard arriving,
mustn't forget to tell Lou.* That was all.

She sighed and closed the book, reflecting that it was
a waste of time having a diary if you couldn't ever find

it and made no effort to use it properly. But at least it gave this strange man with his amused blue eyes some credibility—Neil did know him and had invited him to stay. She stood for a moment, biting her lip, then came to a decision.

'Look—' she walked back into the lounge '—I will put you up for a few days, Mr Moore. My brother can be extremely forgetful at times but you are in his diary.' She gestured a bit helplessly. 'So, apologies on his be-half but if we don't hear from him shortly I would imag-ine that staying any longer would be a waste of your time?'

Richard Moore gave the matter his full consideration for a good half minute, at the same time, unbeknownst to Louise, suppressing an inner desire to laugh at his absolute failure to make any impression on this girl who was now playing the polite hostess—much against her will, he suspected.

And Louise discovered unexpectedly that she was holding her breath and wondered why.

But he said at length, with a charming smile, 'I'd very much appreciate that, Miss Brown.'

'Yes, well,' she responded a touch dryly, 'if you'll come this way, I'll show you the guest room and while you freshen up I'll make some lunch.'

'Please don't go to any trouble on my account, ma'am.'

Louise tossed him a cool glance. 'I was about to make lunch for myself.'

She looked up from the salad she was making half an hour later as her uninvited guest came into the kitchen.

He'd obviously showered and had changed into blue

shorts and a white T-shirt. His thick hair was damp and brushed and he'd shaved. Louise paused in her chopping as they eyed each other in a curiously charged little moment. Then she nodded towards the bundle of clothes he had in his arms. 'Put that in the laundry; I'll deal with it.'

'I can do it. I—'

'If you're anything like Neil, letting you loose in the laundry is inviting disaster,' she said ruefully. 'I'd rather do it myself. The laundry's through there.' She pointed to a doorway. 'Just leave it on the washing-machine. Lunch is ready.'

'Yes, ma'am!' Richard Moore said, and disappeared into the laundry.

Louise stayed where she was for a moment with her knife poised and her eyes narrowed in annoyance. Then she shrugged, inspected her salad and took it over to the table. There was a platter of cold meat, garlic potatoes in their jackets, a dish of rice with capsicum, raisins and nuts and a basket of crunchy bread.

'Would you like a beer or a glass of wine?' she asked as he came back and took the chair she indicated. 'It is Saturday.'

'I'd love a beer.'

Louise poured herself a glass of wine and brought him a beer. The dining alcove adjoined the kitchen and looked out through wooden-framed French doors over a small walled garden with a patch of lawn, flowering creepers, some trees in tubs and a brilliant border of pink and white petunias. 'Cheers. Please help yourself.'

'After you,' he said courteously, and handed her the platter of cold meat. 'May I ask your first name?'

'Louise.'

'And what do you do, Louise?' he said, after waiting a moment.

'I'm a teacher.'

A faint smile tugged at his lips as his leisurely gaze ran over her.

'That amuses you?' she asked tartly.

'It's just—' he shrugged '—that you don't look like one at all. What do you teach?' he asked rapidly, as if to forestall the annoyed response he suspected, correctly as it happened, she might be framing.

Louise's gaze was less than impressed. 'History. And I'm the choirmistress,' she said at length.

He, on the other hand, looked suitably impressed. 'What age group do you take?'

'We have three choirs to take in all ages, and I teach high-school history.'

'You don't look old enough,' he commented.

'To be a high-school teacher?' She smiled briefly. 'I'm twenty-five.'

'Is it a mixed school?'

'No, a private girls' school. Tell me something, Mr Moore.' She frowned. 'What did you and Neil plan to do for a fortnight?'

A keen blue gaze shot her way, then Richard Moore concentrated on his meal again. 'There is a bird here Neil is very interested in. Seems it's getting rarer and rarer. We were hoping to get some pictures so we could put together some kind of a survival programme.'

'What bird?'

'The jabiru.'

'Don't tell me Neil's added that to his list of lame ducks!' Louise said wearily.

Richard Moore laughed spontaneously and after a moment she had to laugh as well.

'Sorry,' she said ruefully, 'but I can tell you that in the last four or five years I've probably seen only that many jabiru in the waterways around here.'

'That's sad.'

'Yes,' she agreed. 'Mind you, when Neil takes up a cause anything can happen. When he remembers, that is.' She stood up, having finished her lunch, but her guest was making a much larger meal. Almost as if he hadn't eaten for days. Can't he even afford to eat? she wondered, and put a basket of fruit on the table. 'Did you have any plans for this afternoon?' she asked as she started to make coffee.

He put his knife and fork together finally. 'Thank you very much for that. No. Well, I was wondering whether you'd mind if I had a sleep? I'm a bit zonked out.'

'Not at all!' Louise stopped and winced inwardly at the undoubted enthusiasm in her voice, but her guest appeared not to notice. 'I've got a few calls to make this afternoon so, no, please feel free,' she said more moderately.

She put a cup of coffee in front of him and encountered a little glint in his eyes that was slightly at odds with the way he thanked her politely, that told her he had noticed her enthusiasm. She felt a tinge of colour stain her cheeks. Damn the man! She tossed her head and started to clear the table.

'Can I give you a hand with the dishes?' he offered. 'I'm quite house-trained.'

'No, I'm fine, thanks.'

'Then would you consider letting me cook you dinner

tonight? I make a mean macaroni cheese.' He chose an orange and started to peel it with his long fingers.

Louise stopped loading the dishwasher and studied him with a frown. 'Are you serious?'

'Yes, ma'am.'

'And you don't burn pots and leave a dreadful mess?'

'I wouldn't dream of it.'

'Well—' she hesitated, then a genuine smile curved her lips '—if you'd really like to, that'd be a first! None of Neil's—er—friends seem capable of boiling water, let alone an egg. I think I've got everything you need.' She opened the pantry cupboard and found a packet of macaroni. 'There's plenty of cheese, there's milk, ham, tomatoes, mustard. Why not?'

'What time would you like to eat?'

'Seven? I'm also going to visit a friend in hospital but I should be back by then.'

'Nothing serious, I hope?'

'Depends on how you look at it,' Louise said wryly. 'She's just had her first baby.'

'Ah.'

'You know about babies?' She shot him a curious look.

'Enough to suspect that after the first bliss they can be exhausting, time-consuming little people who can't talk and tell you what you're doing wrong.'

Louise laughed. 'How right you are. I've seen quite a few friends tearing their hair out over their little bundles of joy—which reminds me, I must get a present.'

Richard Moore stood up, stretched and yawned. 'You're not far from the beach here, are you?'

'Only a couple of blocks.'

'I thought I might go for a swim later.'

'Why don't you?'

'Thank you again for putting me up and feeding me.'

'You're welcome,' Louise said, slowly, because her dining area seemed to have shrunk and it was difficult not to be somewhat overwhelmed by this would-be photographer. She turned away abruptly.

'He's a darling,' Louise said to her best friend, Jane, and handed the baby back. 'I think Bradley suits him beautifully.'

'Of course, it will be Brad,' Jane responded, 'but I don't mind.' She gazed down at her baby with utter devotion, then looked up at Louise a little guiltily. 'So what have you been up to?'

'The same. Well, one of Neil's lame ducks showed up out of the blue.' She explained the circumstances and Jane, who knew Neil, laughed.

'What's he like? As wrapped up in his science as the rest of them?'

'Not really,' Louise said slowly. 'And for some reason I don't feel quite comfortable with him.'

'Why?'

Louise considered. 'I've got the feeling he's laughing at me,' she said with a frown and had the strange thought that she was being toyed with, even. 'Amongst other things.'

'Describe him.'

'Thirty-two, big, tall, attractive in a laid-back kind of way—rather like a well-fed tiger,' she said dryly. 'He can cook, he—'

'Lou! He might be just what you need.'

Louise looked around the flower-filled room then regarded her friend, bedecked in a pretty nightgown and unable to keep her eyes off her baby for any length of time. 'You won't be happy until you see me married and producing babies too, will you?' she said ruefully.

'You are twenty-five,' Jane pointed out.

'Almost over the hill?'

'Of course not but, yes, I would like to see you…in love at least.'

'In case the juices dry up?' Louise suggested wryly.

'Has it—falling in love, I mean—never happened for you?' Jane asked curiously.

Louise paused. 'I thought it might have once but it didn't last the distance.'

'You shouldn't give up trying, though.'

'Trying to fall in love?' Louise looked sceptical.

'I didn't mean that. I meant you shouldn't shut yourself off from the possibility,' Jane corrected her.

Louise laughed. 'Of course I haven't. But I don't think this man is the answer to my prayers, somehow. As a matter of fact, I'm quite happy the way I am, Jane.'

'That's what I'm afraid of,' Jane replied cryptically, but before Louise could take issue young Bradley woke up.

She stayed another hour with her friend, then drove home as the sun set.

She arrived on her doorstep and paused as she put her key into the door to frown at a strange sound coming from within. Almost as if she'd acquired a menagerie. Then silence reigned. She opened the door and her uninvited guest appeared in the hallway.

'Hi,' she said. 'Did you have your sleep and your swim?'

'Hi,' he responded, and leant his shoulder against the

wall. 'I decided to have my swim first but I didn't manage to get a sleep.'

'Oh? That's a pity.' She put her bag down on the hall table. 'You know, I could have sworn I heard—a dog. I must be imagining things.' She grimaced and went to go past him towards the kitchen.

But he said, 'Not one—three.'

She stopped abreast of him. 'What on earth do you mean?'

'They're puppies, actually. They were on the doorstep when I got back from the beach. Together with their owners.'

'*Puppies*?'

'Puppies,' he agreed. 'Three of them. The couple who were with them assured me you would be only too happy to take them in. So they left them with me.'

Louise stared at him wide-eyed.

He straightened, pulled a piece of paper from his pocket and handed it to her. 'They wrote you this note.'

The note read:

Dear Lou, we're at our wits' end. The neighbours are complaining, the landlord threatened to turf us out this morning, nobody seems interested in buying them. Don't forget she had eight! And because we know you work so tirelessly for the RSPCA we felt sure you would be able to find homes for them. Love, Marge and Fred

'I don't believe it,' Louise said, and started to laugh helplessly.

Richard raised an eyebrow. 'You will when you see

them. Is this a common occurrence in the Brown house-hold?'

'No! Well—uh—what have you done with them?'

'After chasing them about the house, cleaning up several messes, rescuing sundry shoes from death by chewing, et cetera, I penned them up in the laundry, fed them copious amounts of bread soaked in milk—and prayed to God they might fall asleep! Can I ask you something? Why would Marge and Fred imagine they could... simply dump them on you out of the blue?'

'Oh, well, it's like this. They're a dear old couple who live in an old house nearby that's divided into four flats. They're pensioners, half-deaf, and their dog, Mitzie, is terribly precious to them. Unfortunately, she got out one night and a couple of weeks later they realized that it must have been quite a night!'

'I see. Where do you come in?'

'Well, I sometimes do their shopping for them and I happened to mention, before the puppies were born, that I might be able to help place them. I didn't hear from Marge and Fred so I thought it had all been taken care of—they *must* have been desperate, poor old souls!'

'And you do work for the RSPCA?'

'Only some fund-raising. You'd better lead me to them!' she said with a grin.

But it was a moment before he led the way, a moment in which he studied her narrowly and curiously. Then, with a shrug, he preceded her to the laundry.

'Oh,' Louise said. 'Oh! This is incredible!'

'I'm in complete agreement,' Richard Moore murmured.

'But, no, what I mean is—you don't know Mitzie! She's quite small whereas these—heaven alone knows

what the father must have been!' She had to raise her
voice above the din as three large puppies yapped and
cried and curled themselves around her feet.

'A Great Dane?' Richard suggested dryly.

'Looking at their paws, you could be right. OK, OK.'
She sank to her knees and allowed herself to be licked
enthusiastically and crawled over. 'Despite your unim-
aginable pedigree you're all gorgeous, I know, but you
don't have to make so much noise! And I would dearly
love to keep you but I've got the strong feeling you're
going to need very big gardens, not to say a farm!' She
turned a laughing face up to Richard Moore. 'I see why
you got no sleep.'

'So you—really don't mind this—imposition?' he said
slowly. 'Why couldn't your neighbours have gone
straight to the RSPCA?'

'They are old.' Louise defended Fred and Marge.
'They'd have got an awful fright, thinking they might
be evicted, and it is a Saturday. But—' she got up '—*I'm*
going to have to do something tonight otherwise *my*
neighbours will be complaining! Now let me think.' She
shooed the puppies from the door and retreated to the
kitchen, closing the door. 'Well, a bit of sweet-talking
may be the way to go. I do know the caretaker of the
shelter—she'll probably come and get them if I go about
it the right way.' She reached for the phone.

An hour later much had been accomplished. The puppies had departed, the laundry had been hosed out,
Marge and Fred had been spoken to and reassured, and
peace reigned once more.

'What I need is a drink,' Richard said ruefully. 'That
was masterly, by the way. You obviously have a real
talent for welfare, especially the organizational side of

it!' He poured two glasses of wine and brought one over to her.

Louise looked at his ruffled hair and said gravely, 'I'm sorry you've had such a disrupted afternoon. Look, don't worry about dinner; we—'

'It's done. Only needs to be heated up. I did it in between—puppy-sitting,' he said ironically.

Louise glanced around the kitchen with widening eyes. It was spotless. 'I think you're in the wrong occupation, Mr Moore!'

'You haven't tasted it yet.'

'The proof will be in the pudding? Why do I get the feeling it'll be a masterpiece?' Louise said wryly.

He shrugged, and the phone rang.

Louise answered it. When she had finished the conversation, despite having offered warm and delighted congratulations to the caller, she put it down looking rueful.

'Mixed news?' Richard suggested, then looked comically apprehensive. 'Not another invasion of domestic life of the untrained variety?'

She chuckled. 'No. I was planning a day out on the boat tomorrow but the couple I invited have had to cancel. You won't believe this but she's just discovered *she's* pregnant. Which explains why she's feeling sick and the thought of being on a boat is anathema at the moment!'

'Why wouldn't I believe it?' he asked with a faint smile.

Louise grimaced. 'What I meant was, *I* can't believe how many of my friends are in the family way.'

'You have no plans in that regard yourself?' he enquired after a moment.

'None.'

'Any special reason?'

She glanced at him fleetingly. 'Yes. No special man, Mr Moore.'

'That could change,' he offered.

'Of course. Until it does, I'm perfectly happy the way I am,' she said with some irony, remembering her conversation with Jane not that long ago.

'That's fine, then,' he murmured, and straightened. 'Why don't you take a break? I'm determined not to have you lifting a finger this evening, cooking or kitchen-wise. I need about twenty minutes to get dinner ready.'

She studied him for a moment, amazed to discover that she felt defensive. As if, she thought, I should be explaining that I'm perfectly normal. Although why I should be on the defensive towards a man I barely know, over an issue that has nothing to do with him, is a—is crazy! 'All right,' she said abruptly. 'I'll leave you to do it.'

But she stayed a moment longer as they stared into each other's eyes. She felt a faint frisson run along her nerve-ends that she realized translated to an inability to be entirely unmoved by this man in a rather specific way. Which was, it shocked her to discover, the strange little conviction that she would very much enjoy having his hands upon her body, his blue eyes narrowed and un-amused, as they made a different kind of acquaintance.

She moved restlessly as an inward tremor of pleasure ran through her. Louise! she immediately mocked herself. He can't be that attractive. Don't forget he is sponging off you at the moment, even if he is a friend of Neil's.

'Give me a call when you're ready,' she said coolly, and took herself off.

She went straight to her piano.

In times of joy, in times of stress it was her release and at all times it was her hobby. She started off with Chopin and was into Brahms' *Lullaby*, dedicated to Jane's little Brad, when Richard came into the lounge and said that dinner was ready.

She took her wine with her and sat down. The macaroni cheese steamed deliciously in a casserole and there was a salad to go with it.

'Mmm…' She breathed in. 'Smells good.'

He dished up two portions, filled her glass and sat down opposite. 'You play beautifully.'

'Thanks. It was my great ambition to be a concert pianist.' She helped herself to salad.

'By the sound of it you might have made it.'

'No.' She shook her head and sipped her wine. 'But I'm not desolated. And I do play in public sometimes. Charity concerts, children's wards, old people's homes, that kind of thing.'

'You really are a do-gooder, Louise.'

'Hardly. This *is* delicious.'

'Thanks. You don't like to talk about it?'

She considered. 'Not much. Neil is the do-gooder in the family. I mean, he achieves things on a global scale.'

'Perhaps you sell yourself short?'

'No. Tell me a bit more about yourself, Richard,' she said, in an obvious bid to change the subject.

He registered this with a faint smile, then shrugged. 'There's not a lot to tell. Uh—I'm not musical, unfortunately, although I enjoy other people's music. I read a lot,' he offered, and returned his concentration to his dinner.

They ate in silence for a while, although Louise registered the fact that she was being deliberately blocked on the subject of getting to know any more about this man. And she remembered that uncomfortable little thought she'd had while she was with Jane—that she was being toyed with. Why do I think that? she wondered. Because he's changed since our first encounter on the doorstep? It's as if he's downplaying himself now. Is he *that* broke?

'Have you—?' She paused. 'I know this could be rather a come-down from wildlife but have you considered fashion photography? It so happens I have a friend who works for a fashion magazine. I could...I could have a word with her if you like. It might be something to tide you over,' she finished with an awkward little shrug.

There was dead silence. Then Richard Moore said with a curious little glint—of affection? Louise wondered—in his eyes, 'Like brother, like sister. I don't think that would suit me, somehow.'

'I have offended you,' she said a little stiffly. 'Sorry, it was only a thought.'

'You haven't offended me at all. I'm just—I don't think I have the temperament for it but thank you very much for the offer. So—you're not going sailing tomorrow?'

She shrugged. 'Doesn't seem much point.'

'Is it hard to handle on your own? The boat?'

She glanced at him with a trace of scorn. 'Not in the least. I was just looking forward to relaxing with some friendly company.'

'I could supply that.'

Louise cursed herself inwardly for not seeing the trap she'd fallen into.

'It is the boat Neil would have been planning to use for jabiru hunting, I presume?' he added.

She glanced at him through her lashes. 'Yes. We own it together. It's highly unlikely we'd see a jabiru tomorrow. Sunday is always busy on the Broadwater.'

'You never know. Neil was quite enthusiastic about our chances of finding some, by the way.'

'Neil is an eternal optimist.'

'So I gathered, but he's very highly regarded in the international conservation movement, you know.'

'I do know,' Louise returned.

'Would it be out of the question to take me sailing tomorrow? It might be as close as I ever get to these jabiru. At least I'll see their habitat,' he said ruefully.

She regarded him expressionlessly for a long moment, then sighed suddenly as her brother's face swam before her eyes again. 'All right. I'm sure Neil would like me to do that for you.'

For some reason he looked distinctly quizzical although he said gravely, 'Thank you, Louise. What time did you have in mind?'

'As early as possible. I like to work the tide. It's also a good time for seeing the birdlife—and there is plenty of it other than jabiru. Say—eight o'clock?'

'Suits me. I'm an early riser.'

Louise pushed her plate away. 'And I'm very full. I think I need a run around the block!'

'Why don't we?'

Louise paused and thought, Why not? 'If you let me help you with the dishes first.'

'That wasn't on the agenda,' he reminded her.

'Take it or leave it, Mr Moore.'

'You drive a hard bargain, Miss Brown. OK!'

They walked the couple of blocks to the beach, took their shoes off and strode out on the firm, damp sand at the water's edge. It was a lovely night, clear and starry, and the lights of Surfers Paradise built magic castles in the air as the surf pounded and ebbed and the spray tasted salty on their lips.

MacRae Place was alive as they walked back. Its restaurants and pavement cafés were busy, there was music on the air and the lit shop fronts—amongst them some exquisite boutiques and interior design studios—were attracting a crowd of window-shoppers.

Much beloved by its locals for its village atmosphere, MacRae Place was a mixture of old and new, as Louise pointed out to Richard Moore as they strolled along. There were some high-rise apartment blocks in the area but there were also old houses, grassy footpaths and trees. And the recent accent was more on low-level developments, such as the town house complex she lived in with its sandy-pink walls and olive-green shutters.

'Can I buy you coffee?' he asked.

'Well—' Louise stopped outside her favourite café and was assailed by the aroma of freshly ground coffee. 'If you like.'

'Here?' He looked around. The café spilt colourfully onto the pavement and there were fairy lights wound into the trees at the road's edge.

'It's my favourite,' she said, and they sat down at a table for two.

'Hi, Miss Brown!' A waitress came over and looked at Richard Moore with patent interest.

Louise smiled a little wryly at the girl. Amy Lewis was a devoted pupil of hers in her last year at school and she waitressed on weekends to earn pocket money. She was also deeply interested in Louise's private life, what there was of it. This titbit that Miss Brown had been seen with a man would be all over the school on Monday, Louise just knew.

'Hello, Amy. How's business tonight?'

'Really busy, Miss Brown, it's such a lovely night!' She smiled beguilingly at Richard, then turned back to Louise, obviously dying to be introduced.

'This is Richard Moore,' Louise said gravely. 'Richard—Amy Lewis, one of my history pupils.'

'I'm nearly finished school,' Amy said hastily, then blushed brightly as Richard stood up to shake her hand.

'Lucky you,' he said. 'How nice to meet you. We're only after coffee, I'm afraid.'

'That's no problem! What would you like? Cappuccino, Vienna, long black, short black...' Amy ran out of coffees and was suddenly tongue-tied and unable to drag her eyes away from Richard.

'Vienna?' Richard asked Louise, who nodded. 'Two, then,' he said to Amy. 'Thank you so much.'

'It's a pleasure,' she breathed, and turned away to all but trip over a tub of flowers.

Louise eyed Richard as he sat down. 'You made a bit of a hit there.'

He looked wry. 'Quite unwittingly. At—eighteen?'

'Eighteen,' Louise agreed.

'Life can be awfully embarrassing, can't it?'

'Don't remind me! Nevertheless, you will be all over

my school on Monday, Mr Moore.' She stared at him solemnly, then her lips twitched.

'Ah. Our names will be romantically linked, you mean?'

'If I know Amy.'

He sat back and studied Louise thoughtfully.

'What now?' she asked.

'It doesn't bother you?'

'No, of course not.' She laughed. 'She's a sweet kid, actually. Got a bit wayward about a year ago but mainly because her parents were having marital problems. I— managed to—' she shrugged '—help a bit.'

'How did you do that?' he asked curiously.

Louise paused. 'It was nothing much. I do a bit of voluntary work at a school for disabled children and I took Amy along. Sometimes it helps to be reminded just how well off you are compared to—others.'

'What if it were true?'

'What?' Louise looked at him enquiringly.

'That we were romantically linked?'

Louise's response was forestalled by the arrival of two Vienna coffees in tall glasses topped with cones of cinnamon-sprinkled cream. Amy, it appeared, had regained her composure—either that or curiosity had got the better of her embarrassment. She'd also applied some bright red lipstick. 'There we go,' she said as she put the glasses down carefully, and drew a pad from her pocket. 'Are you from out of town, Mr Moore?'

'It so happens I am, Amy, and due to be banished back there shortly.' He took the bill and handed her some money.

'Oh, what a shame! I mean—' she turned to Louise

'—you'll probably be disappointed about that, Miss Brown.'

'We barely know each other, Amy,' Louise said calmly. 'Richard is my brother's friend, not mine.'

'Really!' For a moment Amy's eyes lit up but what she would have been prompted to utter next was nipped in the bud by an urgent call from her employer. 'Got to go, sorry.' And she *did* trip over the tub of flowers this time.

'Do you always have this effect on women?' Louise asked.

'Obviously not,' he replied. 'You haven't tripped once since we met.'

'Perhaps I'm a bit of a tough nut?' Louise suggested, and her green gaze was suddenly ironic.

'I didn't say that—'

'I know, I said it.' She looked amused.

'And are you?' he asked after a moment.

Louise paused to consider, then she grimaced. 'I don't think I'm the soft, cuddly type.'

It was his turn to look amused. 'That can be quite a recommendation.'

'Can it?' She looked thoughtful. 'I was once led to believe otherwise but—' she smiled fleetingly '—to be trite, it probably takes all types. So you don't like your women soft and cuddly?'

As soon as the words left her mouth, she wished she'd never uttered them and looked at him with a spark of embarrassment. 'Don't answer. I don't really want to know. I'm much more interested in why— No, strike that as well,' she murmured, and took refuge in her coffee.

'Why I'm thirty-two and not making much of my life?' he suggested with a wicked little grin.

'It's crossed my mind,' she admitted, reddening, and hesitated before she added, 'Would I be right in thinking you're a bit of a loner?'

'What makes you think that?'

'You're not very forthcoming about yourself.'

He grimaced. 'Perhaps I am.'

'Have you ever *tried* another kind of job?'

'I—' He paused and stirred the bottom of his glass. 'I seem to have an inner resistance to a nine-to-five kind of existence.'

'But one can't go on for ever like a hermit crab,' she objected. 'Can one?'

A faint smile touched his mouth. 'Some do. Like you,' he added with a sudden gravity that was entirely assumed, 'I'm perfectly happy the way I am.'

'When did I say that?'

'When you were explaining the lack of a man in your life.'

Louise bit her lip and shrugged. 'Oh, well— Look, please let me pay for my coffee. I always believe in going Dutch. And if we're going to get an early start perhaps we should think of bed?'

'Why not?' He stood up. 'But I wouldn't dream of letting you pay for your coffee.'

'I—'

'I'm not completely broke, Miss Brown,' he assured her.

To her dismay, Louise twisted and turned for a while before she fell asleep. And all because she couldn't stop

thinking about Richard Moore, no doubt sleeping peacefully one floor down from her.

A strange little feeling of tension had gripped her
when they'd got home. As she'd gone around closing
curtains and locking up, she'd felt his presence strongly,
although he'd stayed in the kitchen unloading the dishwasher. Nor had he made any attempt to delay her; in
fact he'd wished her goodnight simply and gone to bed
first.

What was I expecting? she wondered. I'd have fought
tooth and nail if he'd made one move. So *why* do I feel
slightly let down? It surely couldn't have anything to do
with the way Amy was simply bowled over!

She turned over and punched her pillow. And was
struck again by the two distinct impressions she had of
Richard Moore. That first one when she could have
sworn he was an authoritative man who didn't suffer
fools gladly—and the placid, secretly amused one he'd
presented ever since.

Not only that, she thought with further irritation,
there's the fact that he's a self-confessed loner who
doesn't seem to care much that he's thirty-two and de-
pending on Neil to give his career a boost!

She stared into the darkness for a while and then
thought, with a touch of wry humour, The sooner he
goes the better. A hermit who attracts women the way
he does is the last thing I need in my life.

CHAPTER TWO

'HAVE you ever sailed before?'

'A bit.'

Louise raised an eyebrow.

'Have I said something wrong?' Richard enquired.

'No. Well, I'm always a bit wary of people who have sailed "a bit".'

'Shall I just do what I'm told, then?'

'If you wouldn't mind.'

'Aye, aye, skipper!' He touched a hand to his cap.

'If you're laughing at me,' Louise began, 'I—'

'Wouldn't dream of it,' he broke in gravely.

'All the same, I know you are,' she said hotly.

'Louise,' he replied firmly, 'let's get under way, shall we? It's a beautiful morning and far too early to be wrangling over nuances.'

She eyed him in his blue shorts and white T-shirt, his peaked cap that said 'SAVE THE RHINO' on it, and the whole impressive, lazy length of him, only to have him return her gaze candidly as he looked from her tied-back hair, her pink blouse and shorts and down the length of her legs. She turned away abruptly.

It was a beautiful morning. The early sunlight was dancing on the mirror-like surface of the Broadwater, gulls were wheeling white in the blue of the sky and the air was warm and salty.

The Southport Yacht Club marina was within walking distance of MacRae Place and was where she and Neil

33

berthed the *Georgia 2*. On this Sunday morning, it was coming alive with the prospect of a perfect day on the water. There were sleek ocean-going yachts cheek by jowl with powerful motor boats. There were fly-bridge cruisers, catamarans and home-made boats tied up to its extensive network of jetties. There were excited children on the walkways, and yachting dogs, as she thought of them—because so many yachties seemed to have their dogs living on board with them, dogs that handled themselves like seasoned sailors.

A thirty-two-foot motor sailor, the *Georgia 2* was a trim little craft that combined power and sail. It had a comfortable back deck area, a neat main cabin and galley, and four bunks. The drive station was covered overhead and the hull was a spanking white. The decks were inlaid teak, the woodwork was varnished and the brass fittings were polished and shining.

'You're right,' Louise said suddenly, turning back. 'If you cast off, I'll drive out.'

She negotiated the marina successfully and got them into the main channel. 'Don't think we'll bother with the sail yet,' she called to him. 'There's not enough breeze.'

He climbed down into the cockpit. 'Wouldn't blow out a candle,' he agreed. 'You've got some power.'

'A forty horsepower diesel,' she told him. And, because she felt a bit guilty about how she'd started out the morning, added, 'Like to take the wheel?'

For a moment he looked at her as if he was going to say something along the lines of, Sure you trust me? But as she read his mind and her lips quivered he merely said, 'Love to.'

'OK. Green to port, red to starboard until we get to

the Seaway; it's quite simple.' She handed over the wheel.

A few minutes later she could see that Richard Moore was very much at home and seemed to know what he was doing as he negotiated several trawlers coming home from a night's fishing. I might have known, she thought ruefully, but said, 'What would you give for a cup of tea and a muffin?'

'Quids!'

'So would I.' She climbed down into the cabin and set the kettle onto a gas stove. She'd got up at the crack of dawn and cooked a chicken for lunch, and she put it and the salad she'd made into the small fridge. She popped the muffins into the oven while the kettle boiled, and when they came out warm she split them and buttered them generously. Then she carried them and two mugs of strong tea up to the deck.

'I was just going to give you a shout. This is a bit confusing,' he said.

'Ah.' Louise shaded her eyes with her hand and looked around. The Seaway that led out to the ocean was on their starboard hand. 'See those yellow buoys? They're west cardinal marks. Keep them to starboard and they'll take you past the Seaway. That's Wavebreak Island.' She pointed to the island on their left with its fringe of casuarinas. 'Then from there on the channel is marked for the port of Brisbane, red to port, green to starboard.'

'Got you.'

'Would you like to see a chart? Then you'll know exactly where you are.'

'Yes, but have your tea first. There's no hurry.' He picked up a muffin.

Louise sat down on a deck-chair and took up her mug.

'This is the life,' Richard said with a grin.

'You're right.' She grinned back. 'I know a lovely place to have a swim and lunch. We might even see a jabiru.'

'I thought that was highly unlikely.'

'I've just got the feeling anything's possible today,' she murmured with a shrug, and paused to examine this feeling of well-being she suddenly had. It was true she loved the boat. True that nobody in their right mind could take issue with the day, but where had all her uncertainty of the night before and her tendency of the morning to take offence vanished to?

She sipped her tea and watched Richard as he handled the controls. He was standing at the wheel, leaning against a bulwark with his arms folded, his eyes narrowed against the sun, and every now and then he put a hand on the wheel to adjust their course. His feet were bare and his long legs covered in golden hairs.

It occurred to Louise to wonder again what kind of a man he really was. You couldn't deny that the hermit label sat well on him this morning. You could, at this moment, visualize him being perfectly content to sail the *Georgia 2* off into the sunset. So why did she have the strong feeling there was a lot more to him?

Unless it was wishful thinking?

Possibly, she conceded to herself. You'd like to invest him with a bit more substance, wouldn't you? Then you could feel happier about—what? That incredible little rush of sheer physical attraction you experienced last night?

'Penny for them?'

'Oh! Sorry, I was miles away,' she replied untruthfully to his query and sat up, put her mug down and chose a muffin. 'We're going past Runaway Bay at the moment, on the left. And, of course, that's South Stradbroke Island on our right. It, North Stradbroke and Moreton Island are what give the Broadwater and Moreton Bay their protection from the open sea. By the way, where do you come from? In case I'm initiating the initiated.'

'You're not. Oh, I've been to the Gold Coast before but never on the waterways. Uh…Sydney. I learnt to sail on the harbour, then did a bit of offshore sailing round there.'

'No wonder! I've heard that's pretty tricky.'

'It can be. Not, naturally, as protected as these waters.'

'A *bit*,' Louise said reflectively. 'You might have told me.'

'It's your boat. I can't stand people who jump on board and immediately want to take over.'

She laughed. 'How right you are.' She stood up and opened a cupboard. 'Here's the chart. We're here. And this is where I thought of having lunch. Jumpinpin. See the bar between North and South Stradbroke? Well, this side of it is beautiful. Clear, clear water, lovely sand, birds galore. It'll take us about two hours to get there.'

'Sounds ideal.'

It was ideal.

They anchored in a shallow bay adjacent to Jumpinpin bar where the sand was white, the water turquoise and they could see huge flocks of wading birds on the low dunes of the narrow point of the island. There was an intoxicating feeling of space, a huge sky and the ocean side of the island was within walking distance.

Louise stripped off her shorts and blouse to reveal a pink bikini and dived off the duckboard. The water was delicious and so clear, she could see the sandy bottom. Two minutes later, Richard followed her in.

'See what I mean?' she called as he swam past her. 'Isn't it divine?'

'Magic,' he agreed, coming up with his hair plastered to his head.

They swam for a while, then she suggested they walk so they got themselves caps and shirts from the boat, stuck the shirts under their caps and paddled to the shore. 'We'll cook if we don't put them on,' Louise said, retrieving her shirt from under her cap as she stood up on the beach. 'Let's go and have a look at the bar.'

Richard dragged his shirt on and repositioned his 'rhino' cap. As they went, she told him the history of Jumpinpin bar and how North and South Stradbroke had been one island originally until the narrow neck joining them had been breached.

'It's incredible,' he said as they watched the jumbled waters and sandbanks of the bar, too treacherous to negotiate except with a lot of local knowledge. He gazed around at the Pacific surf pounding the ocean side of the island. 'So close to the glitter of Surfers and the Gold Coast, but you could be on an uninhabited island a million miles away.'

Louise glowed. 'It's one of my favourite spots. And you're right, it's amazing to be able to get such a feeling of unspoiled wilderness so close to home. A lot of people don't realize what the Gold Coast has to offer, you know. It's not all high-rise and glitz.'

He glanced down at her. 'I wouldn't have taken you for a wilderness girl.'

'Then I'm glad I've proved you wrong. You shouldn't make snap judgements about people.'

'I don't, usually,' he said wryly, 'and I didn't mean to offend you.'

'You didn't really.' She started to walk again. 'So you're very much a wilderness man?'

'At times.'

'And in between times?'

'Pretty much the same as any other guy, I guess.'

She laughed. 'What a cop-out! Never mind, I won't pry any more.' She stopped, swung her arms in a wide arc and looked at him sideways. 'Tell you what I will do—I'll race you back to the boat.'

'All the way?'

'All the way. First to touch the duckboard is the winner.'

'You're on. I'll give myself a count to twenty handicap.'

'Are you going to regret that, Mr Moore?' she teased as she pulled off her shirt and stuck it under her cap, and sprinted off. But instead of taking the beach way they'd come she ran over a low dune, splashed into the lagoon and started to do a strong breast-stroke to approach the boat from a different angle—a longer swim but easier than running over the hot sand. She was a very good swimmer.

And she won the race, but only just. He put his hand on the duckboard moments after her.

'Not bad, Mr Moore, not bad at all,' she said between breaths, and laughed as she tossed her cap and shirt onto the back deck.

'And very clever, Miss Brown,' he returned as they rested side by side in the water. 'Not only that. You wouldn't have had the ambition to be an Olympic swimmer by any chance?'

Louise floated on her back, letting the turquoise water caress her body. 'No. But I was a high-school champion. You must be pretty good yourself. Wow! I think that's my exercise for the day.'

'Mine too.'

But as she went to pull herself out of the water their bodies brushed and she stilled as she looked into his eyes. Not only that, she felt herself break out in goosebumps at the contact and didn't feel much inclined to move away. Not, she thought, that it was so surprising. Richard Moore, all sleek and wet and golden, was enough to take your breath away.

Oh, Amy, she reflected, thinking back to the café the night before. I was a bit superior about the way you fell for him on the spot. What price my superiority now, though?

'Would you like a hand?' he murmured, and without waiting for an answer he grasped her lightly around the waist and lifted her out of the water to sit her on the duckboard.

'Thanks.' She got up, put her hands on her hips and stared down at him. 'But there was no need.'

He laughed up at her. 'Sorry. Won't make that mistake again.'

Louise found herself feeling a bit ridiculous and took refuge in drying herself off and wringing out her hair. Then she decided to make amends. 'I have a special ceremony for this kind of day, this *time* of day and it being a Sunday,' she told him confidentially, leaning over the transom.

'What might that be, Miss Brown?'

'One to be taken very seriously.'

He blinked, shook himself, then hauled himself up. 'You've got me worried. You wouldn't be planning to keelhaul me home?'

She smiled ruefully and handed him a towel. 'There is always that, of course, if you misbehave, but no, it's something else. A libation, actually.'

'Ah. Good thinking. What did you have in mind?'

'A gin and tonic before lunch.' She grinned. 'Only one, mind!'

'Definitely. Shall I make them?'

'Yes. I'll get us some nibbles.'

'No jabiru but I can see plenty of wimbrills,' Richard said idly as they sipped their drinks. He reached for an olive. He was sitting on the deck, propped against a stanchion with his legs stretched out and his cap tilted down over his eyes. 'The birdlife is pretty fantastic up here.'

Louise lay back in a deck-chair. She'd put on a filmy white blouse and a big straw sun-hat trimmed with pink roses. It was very hot. 'I do know. Are you itching to photograph it?'

He cast her an amused little glance. 'Not right at the moment. I'm enjoying your Sunday ceremony too much.'

'Good. Now, if this part of the world lives up to its reputation, we should get a bit of a breeze this afternoon. And if the forecast is correct and it's a northerly or a nor'-easterly we may just be able to sail home.'

'Do you ever stay out overnight?'

'Of course.'

'And you don't worry about undesirable elements sneaking aboard and kidnapping you?'

She laughed. 'I wouldn't be easy to kidnap. I've done some karate.'

'You seem to have had a remarkably well-rounded education,' he commented amusedly.

Louise laughed. 'Dad used to say he deplored helpless women. He taught me. He also taught me to sail.'

'And your mother?'

Louise squinted up at him. 'She died when I was six.'

'So you had a far more masculine influence in your life?'

'Yep. Dad also used to say that anything Neil could do I could do, and he was mostly right.' She paused and looked sad. 'He died four years ago.'

'I'm sorry.'

'Thanks. Do you have parents alive?'

'Yes. Both.'

'Do you see much of them?'

'Not a lot— Look at those pelicans.' He pointed and Louise turned her head to smile as two huge pelicans waddled along the beach.

They were quiet for a while, then she said, 'Ready for lunch?'

He smiled at her in a way that did strange things to the pit of her stomach. 'Always.'

Over lunch they chatted—almost, she thought, as if they'd known each other for years. An easy, friendly flow of conversation that took in books, the lighter side of world affairs, cuisine, music. And she told him that despite sometimes having an allergic reaction to Neil's burning passion for conservation it was her ambition to accompany him on one of his expeditions to Africa one day.

'I'm surprised he hasn't taken you already,' Richard said idly.

'Well, I didn't want it to be a short trip. I'd like to take a few months, which means I need to accumulate leave. It'll happen,' she assured him, and was hit by an urgent burst of inspiration. 'That's where you should go! Has Neil said anything about—? Look, if he ever does remember to come home, I'll mention it to him and make *sure* he doesn't forget it. Not that I can promise anything, but there could just be a place for a photographer on his next expedition.'

Richard Moore said nothing for a time, his blue gaze oddly curious as it rested on her eager expression. But he spoke wryly. 'Thank you. Do you always take your brother's lame ducks to heart like this?'

Louise sat back with a grimace. 'I'm told I tend to overdo my desire to…want to help.'

'Neil tells you this?'

She nodded gloomily but said with an imp of mischief, 'I tell him that's a fair case of the pot calling the kettle black. He's the one who finds them in the first place!'

'But you obviously don't confine yourself to them. I've witnessed animal welfare at first hand, you mentioned disabled children, then there's Amy, not to mention Fred and Marge.'

'I'm probably just an interfering busybody!' She gestured casually.

'You seem to be pretty much of a sheet anchor for your brother Neil on the other hand,' he said musingly then.

'I have no idea how he'd cope without me,' she responded with a grin. 'I mean, he might drive me mad from time to time but if he didn't have one single, sane place to come home to—can you imagine?'

Richard laughed. 'He's very lucky. How about another swim?'

They did just that, then, as the breeze got up, weighed anchor and set sail for home.

In the event, it proved to be quite an exciting sail as the breeze strengthened. Louise handled the wheel and Richard handled the sails, and the *Georgia 2* skimmed across the water.

Then things were made more exciting as dark, boiling cloud obscured the sunset and flashes of lightning lit the sky.

'We'll just make it,' Louise called. 'That's quite a storm coming!'

'Yes. Reckon we should reef in?'

'Definitely! Need a hand? I can put her on auto-pilot.'

'No, I can manage. You just get us home as fast as you can,' he called back over the rising wind.

'Aye, aye, skipper!'

But they were only halfway home when the conditions worsened. The wind swung round to a south-easterly, so they were punching into it and it was whipping up quite a swell. And the pyrotechnics of the storm were awesome. Then it started to rain heavily as well as hail.

'We're not going to make it; I can't see a thing! Come under cover,' Louise yelled over the cacophony.

'What do you suggest?' he asked, dropping down beside her as she wrestled with the wheel.

'This is the worst storm I've seen for years,' she answered, peering through the darkness and the teeming rain as hailstones bounced off the roof. 'I think I'm going to have to seek some shelter. But the problem is to find the channel markers, because if we don't we'll run aground. Oh!' She hung onto the wheel as they hit quite a wave.

'Where's the nearest shelter?' he asked as the *Georgia 2* shuddered and ploughed bravely on.

'The lee of Sovereign Island. It'll protect us from the wind and there's deepish water close in. Deep enough for us to anchor, at least. Hell,' she said, and laughed as a green light loomed out of the darkness on their port bow. 'The problem is also to *miss* the channel markers.' She swung the wheel to starboard.

Richard glanced down at her. They were both drenched but there was no doubt that Louise Brown was not scared. Exhilarated, if anything. So, he thought, you're as brave and competent as you're beautiful, Miss Brown. He said, 'I think the hail has stopped and it's not raining quite so hard. What say I go up front as a spotter?'

'Good thinking,' Louise replied. 'But listen, hold on for dear life because the wind hasn't abated and it's really whipping things up. Now, if I'm right, we've got three more green lights to pass to port. Then you should look for a red light and a yellow one in the water; it's a buoy as opposed to a pole. That's the entrance I need to find Sovereign Island. I'm going to put the spotlight on, too.'

But another wave caught the boat abeam, rocking them mightily, and it took all her strength to bring it back on course.

'Look,' she panted. 'I've had second thoughts. You take the wheel, I'll do the spotting. I know what I'm looking for anyway and you've got to be stronger than I am.'

'Oh, no, you don't!' he countered. 'The last thing I need is to lose you overboard, so—'

'Don't argue, Mr Moore,' Louise commanded, and opened a locker to pull out two life-jackets. 'This one's got a lead on it that I can clip to the mast. I'll be quite safe providing you don't tip the boat over. And put this on just in case.'

The next moment she was gone, clambering across the roof of the cabin. Richard Moore cursed beneath his breath but did as he was bid.

And slowly, following Louise's directions as she clung to the mast, he manhandled the *Georgia 2* through the wildest water that had been seen on the Broadwater for years, until they found some shelter, as she'd predicted, in the lee of Sovereign Island.

'Well done!' Louise complimented as she climbed back into the cockpit. The anchor was down and they were riding in relatively calm water, although the storm still raged. 'Did I say something this morning about these *protected* waterways? But I can assure you, this is very unusual.' She laughed up at him with water streaming off her.

'So are you, Louise, so are you,' he said slowly as he helped her out of her life-jacket. And, as if it was the most natural thing in the world, he took the wet, lovely length of her into his arms.

It never occurred to Louise to question what followed. To be kissed by Richard Moore turned out to be an electrifying event—as if all that dynamic electricity had come down from the heavens above to flow between them...

They broke apart to catch their breath and she stared

at him with widening eyes because she'd never before been so aware of a man, never before felt such a flame of desire running through her. And there was no way, nor did she even try, to hide her state of arousal from him—the way her skin trembled at his touch, the way she was captured by that blue gaze and the feel of the strong length of him against her suddenly so-sensitive body.

A clap of thunder rent the air, the boat rocked and he steadied them as the ceiling lamp swayed and washed old-gold light over them. She breathed deeply and he ran his fingers through her dripping hair. They smiled ruefully at each other, but to be wet and clean and cool only heightened the awareness and her smile faded as he drew her closer—because she was longing to dispense with the clinging blouse which was all she had on over her pink bikini.

A brilliant flash of lightning illuminated the shoreline of Sovereign Island and they tensed involuntarily, then clung together as another, deafening clap of thunder broke right over them—and their own storm flared up again.

She shook out her wet hair and leant back against the circle of his arms. He bent his head and kissed the slender line of her throat and she ran her hands over his shoulders. He took a hand from her waist and pushed aside the collar of her blouse, and she took a hand from his shoulder and fumbled the buttons undone. It was the most intense pleasure to feel his lips moving down towards her breasts and her nipples flared into aching peaks beneath the thin silk of her bikini top.

Through all that followed, they said not one word as the storm crashed above them.

*　　*　　*

'You wouldn't believe it could be so calm after last night,' Louise murmured as she steered the *Georgia 2* through an apricot-coloured dawn towards the Southport Yacht Club.

The water was like a millpond, although there was a lot of debris in it from the series of storms that had raged until the early hours.

'No.' They were sipping coffee and Richard glanced at her taut back from where he sat on the deck-chair.

'It's always on the cards at this time of the year, though,' she went on presently. 'Once summer comes in, so do the storms. Although it's only late October, which is a little earlier than normal. Perhaps we're going to have an extra long, hot summer.'

'Perhaps. Louise—'

But she turned to him briefly. 'If you wouldn't mind getting the lines and the fenders ready, we're only about ten minutes out of the marina. Sorry to rush you but I've got to be at school at eight-fifteen.'

'It's only six-thirty now,' he said quietly.

'All the same.'

'OK.' He put down his cup and went to attend to the lines.

There was a surprise waiting for them on the jetty—Neil.

Louise closed her eyes briefly as she made out the agitated figure of her brother and thought, That's all I need.

'Look, I can't tell you how sorry I am,' Neil Brown said for about the tenth time when they were all back at the town house and Richard was cooking breakfast.

Neil was tall, thin, dark and intense. At thirty-one,

he'd never shown the slightest intention of marrying, though not for the lack of women interested in him. Louise sometimes wondered if it was his combination of naïvety and fire that attracted them. Perhaps they thought they could direct that fire towards themselves, she'd pondered occasionally. Little did they know that actually living with him would be a nightmare. Or know the lengths he went to to evade their clutches. Perhaps I make it too easy for him, she'd also pondered.

'I can't imagine how I came to forget,' he added with genuine perplexity.

Louise looked away and happened to catch Richard's eye, which caused her lips to twitch involuntarily as he said gravely, 'I guess we all forget things.'

'What, as a matter of interest, made you remember?' she queried ironically.

'I was having this really interesting discussion with, well, with someone I happened to meet, about a wildlife programme they'd seen on television. Africa and the Serengeti. I'd seen it too, you see, and I suddenly remembered that I knew the person who'd made it. Which, by a natural progression, led me to think, Oh, bloody hell! What date is it today?'

Louise frowned but Neil went on, 'And then to come home and find you gone, Lou, and the boat! I'm a nervous wreck. You should have left a message,' he said reproachfully to his sister.

Louise looked heavenwards this time. 'Talk about the pot calling the kettle black! I wasn't *expecting* to be out overnight. And least of all was I expecting you to suddenly remember your obligations.'

Neil smote his brow, then smiled ingenuously around. 'Never mind, I'm here now. Did Richard tell you we're

mounting a campaign to save the jabiru? If anyone can
achieve it, he can. Mind you, it's also going to be a bit
of a holiday. That's what I promised you, mate, and
that's what I aim to provide. What a pity you're not on
holiday, Lou,' he said regretfully to his sister.

Louise put down her knife and fork with half her perfectly cooked bacon and egg uneaten. She was dressed
and ready to go. She wore a charcoal linen suit with a
short-sleeved but longline jacket over an amber blouse
and straight skirt. Her tights were pale and sheer and she
had on polished black shoes with medium heels. Her hair
was swept back into a severe pleat. A black shoulder
bag hung from her chair and a briefcase rested against
the wall behind her.

Whilst she'd showered, changed and organized herself
hastily for the day, with a mind functioning less than
brilliantly, Neil and Richard had spent the time in the
kitchen. What had she imagined they would be arrang-
ing? she wondered now. Not *this*, surely?

'You mean it's still on?' she said slowly.

'Of course!' Neil blinked at her in the infuriating way
he had when things were quite clear to him but an absolute fog to everyone else. Then he twisted round to
Richard. '*You're* on, aren't you? I mean, I haven't irre-
trievably damned myself, have I?'

Richard paused in the act of flipping an egg, then
looked up and straight at Louise. 'I guess it's up to
Louise,' he said quietly. 'It's her home, too.'

'Oh, that's no problem, then.' Neil heaved a relieved
sigh. 'Lou never minds accommodating guests and you
two must know each other pretty well now. Especially
a guest who can cook. Now that has to be a first, doesn't
it?' he said impishly. 'Lou?'

'Uh—yes,' she replied tonelessly. 'Look, I'm sorry but I'll have to dash.' She pushed her plate away and stood up. 'See you later.'

It was a tiresome day at school.

The choir, which she was coaching for the end-of-year concert, persistently sang out of key and her senior history pupils were tense and fractious with the prospect of exams looming. Or is it me? she stopped to ask herself once. I'm hardly a model of serenity.

She got home at about four o'clock—to an empty house. She breathed a sigh of relief, and changed into shorts and a T-shirt and released her hair. Then she made herself a cup of tea and sat down at the dining table to correct some essays on the French Revolution. It was a hot, steamy afternoon and once she stopped to lift her hair off her neck.

Then she forced herself to concentrate and didn't hear the front door open. So she was unaware that Richard had arrived home, apparently alone, until she looked up suddenly to see him watching her from the doorway.

'Oh. It's you,' she said, trying to recover from the nervous start that had caused her to drop her pen. 'How long have you been there?'

He'd been leaning his shoulders against the doorframe and he straightened slowly. He had on a pair of light khaki trousers, a short-sleeved maroon and green checked shirt and a new pair of desert boots. In fact, she thought, everything looked new and his hair had been trimmed. He said, 'About a minute, Louise. You were obviously engrossed but I didn't meant to startle you.'

'You didn't—I mean, you did, but— What have you been doing?' she said, closing her eyes frustratedly.

'Some much needed shopping.' He pulled out a chair opposite her. 'Then I had lunch with Neil and his girl-friend.'

'His *girlfriend*! I didn't know he had one.'

He shrugged. 'They've been together in the wilds of East Gippsland, apparently, bird-watching.'

Louise stared at him with wide eyes. 'That doesn't sound like Neil. He spends a lot of his time escaping from would-be girlfriends. What's she like?'

Richard considered, then his lips twitched and finally he grinned. 'If you like your women loquacious but plain, she fits the bill completely.'

Louise's lips parted. 'Are you sure she's not an-other—I mean to say—academic or—?'

'You mean to say another lame duck?' he inserted with some irony. 'In fact she's the opposite,' he con-tinued, giving Louise no time to respond. 'But yes, she is an academic. An ornithologist.'

Louise blinked rapidly, then threw tact to the winds. 'How can you be so sure she's not another lame duck?'

'She's the sole heiress to a toilet paper fortune.'

They stared at each other until Louise dissolved into helpless laughter despite herself. 'I don't believe it,' she said at last, wiping her eyes. '*How* plain?'

'Perhaps I was a little unkind there,' Richard said. 'I think she's one of those girls who doesn't believe in gilding the lily at all. On the other hand,' he said medita-tively, 'she may just have the intuition to know that your brother Neil has a habit of running a mile from ultra-feminine women.'

'How right you are,' Louise said slowly, and looked at him with a frown in her eyes. 'You must know him pretty well.'

Richard shrugged.

'What's her name?'

'Eve Parker.'

Louise raised an eyebrow. 'Never heard of them.'

He smiled, a trace wryly, she thought, but couldn't see why. He said, 'We've been invited to have dinner with them.'

'Dinner... Where's she staying? Don't tell me he's bringing her here? I mean—'

'No. She's staying at the Sheraton Mirage, but Neil suggested the café where we had coffee the night before last, because you like it so much there.'

Louise rubbed her face suddenly. 'Why didn't Neil tell me all this himself?'

Richard looked at her steadily. 'He may not have got the chance, this morning.'

Louise lowered her lashes.

'Neither,' he said quietly, 'did I get the time nor was I given the opportunity to at least discuss—'

'I don't think there's anything to discuss.' Louise wrote something in the margin of the book she was correcting, closed it and put it on the pile.

He was silent but when she glanced at him she saw him watching her curiously and ironically.

'I mean—' she swallowed and ran a hand through her hair '—it was the storm and we—just got a bit carried away, don't you think?' She frowned at something in the distance, then looked at him with her green eyes wary and troubled.

'The storm certainly accounted for a part of it,' he agreed. 'But I can't help wondering whether you make a habit of—loving your men so very passionately before banishing them, Louise.'

'You don't seem to be banished,' she retorted.

'Not for the want of wishing it on me,' he murmured wryly in reply.

'I...' Louise looked away tensely. 'I didn't say a word.'

'You didn't have to. You left me in no doubt you were appalled that I hadn't decided to banish myself.'

She switched her gaze back to him. 'I'm sure it was just one of those things so...' She shrugged.

'On the other hand,' he said slowly, and lifted an amused eyebrow at her, 'it would have been hardly chivalrous to just walk away.'

'Not when you know very well it's something I would never have done in—normal circumstances?'

'Do I know that?' he mused. 'I'll tell you what I could be forgiven for thinking—that I'm simply not good enough for you, in your estimation, Miss Brown.'

As this shot landed home with the unerring aim of a well-placed arrow, Louise couldn't help flinching visibly. Something he obviously noted, as a challenging little glint combined with a hint of mockery beamed her way.

'Well, let's look at that,' Louise shot back, recovering some spirit. 'Since you brought it up. You're a complete mystery man, in my humble estimation,' she said sardonically. 'All I really know about you is that you learnt to sail on Sydney Harbour and you met Neil photographing rhinos! Even you must see that's very little to go on.'

'Other than that you loved certain things—'

'Stop it,' Louise said angrily, although there was an unconscious little plea in her voice too, and she stood up. 'You've deliberately evaded telling me anything about yourself.'

'What would you like to know?'

'Nothing. If it has to be drawn out like teeth, nothing!' She gathered her books up.

'All right.' He stood up and handed her the top book that had slid off the pile. 'I hope you didn't fail this poor kid because you're in a temper, Louise?' His blue eyes were alight with wicked amusement now.

She ground her teeth.

'Do you really want me to go?' he said then. 'I could have myself mysteriously called away if you like. If you'd rather your brother remained in ignorance,' he added dryly.

'I'd much rather my brother remained in ignorance—'

'Yes, I can see that. It would be a little difficult to explain things to him, wouldn't it?' His eyes mocked her.

Louise breathed erratically and came to a sudden decision. 'Stay by all means,' she invited. 'It doesn't matter one way or the other to me in the slightest.'

'In that case—' his lips twitched '—why don't you come and have a swim? You look as if you could do with one,' he added candidly.

'Thank you, no. I'm going to water my garden.' She swung on her heel.

'Neil suggested we meet at the café at seven o'clock, by the way,' he said from behind her. 'I gather he's both longing to but curiously shy about introducing you to Eve Parker.'

Louise swung back with a frown. 'Where is he? Why *am* I getting all this second-hand?'

'No great mystery,' Richard replied. 'He's taken Eve

down to the Currumbin Bird Sanctuary. I merely thought
to take some of the element of surprise out of it all for
you.'

'Oh. Well, thanks,' Louise said stiffly.

'You'll come for dinner?'

'Of course I'll come for dinner,' Louise said irritably.
'Heaven alone knows what a mad zoologist and a *plain*
ornithologist could get up to. Not to mention yourself,
Mr Moore,' she added with very genuine exasperation
as she walked away.

She left Richard staring after her with a reluctant grin
twisting his lips before the sudden, all-too-clear recollection of the night before came back to him. This sobered him and he found himself wondering what he had
expected the outcome of the night to be. Not this utter
blank wall, almost as if she's in a state of complete
shock, he mused. Not after...the way it was. Does she
really expect me to simply walk away? If so, why?
Because she *does* think I'm a lame duck?

He narrowed his eyes then smiled, but unamusedly.

As well as the courtyard off the dining area, Louise had
a small front garden behind a high wall with a wrought-
iron gate onto the street. There was a paved area with a
wooden outdoor seat beneath a cream canvas awning,
some velvety lawn and lots of flowers in borders.

She raked the lawn first, then got the hose out and
watered diligently, bending now and then to pluck out
any offending weeds. She gave the pretty little statue of
a naked lady sitting demurely beneath a camellia bush a
cooling shower, and picked some camellias as well as
pruning off the dead heads.

Finally, as dusk fell, her garden was entirely to her

satisfaction and the turmoil of her thoughts had somewhat eased.

She went inside, put the camellias in a glass vase and
carried them up to her bedroom. There was no sign of
Richard Moore and because his bedroom door was open
she assumed he'd gone for a swim.

But as she closed her bedroom door against the world
the thought of him knifing through the surf came to her
and she closed her eyes and leant back against the door
with the vase cradled to her. How could I? she wondered, lifting the creamy blooms and burying her suddenly hot face in amongst them. It seemed so…natural.
It didn't require…conversation. It didn't require expla-
nations or definitions. It was just like the storm—it blew
up out of nowhere.

Until this morning, that is, she reminded herself, pushing away from the door and putting the vase down carefully on her dressing table. Then she studied herself in
the mirror for a while, until she heard the front door
open and close. She snatched her guilty thoughts back
to the present and went to take a shower in her *en suite*
bathroom.

She got downstairs at ten to seven, wearing a long,
silky skirt, white with topaz flowers on it, and a topaz
waistcoat top. Her ash-blonde hair was loose, showing
its slight natural curl as it fell to about six inches below
her shoulders and she had a pair of white backless sandals on. Her expression was inscrutable, however, as
Richard rose politely from a green settee and offered her
a drink. He was in his new clothes.

'No, thanks. I think I'll wait. I am a working girl, after
all,' she said coolly.

'Surrounded by dilettantes?' he suggested gravely.

'It certainly feels that way at times,' she agreed.

'Point taken,' he murmured, but appeared entirely unperturbed.

'Shall we go, then?'

'If I could show you something before we do?'

Louise looked at him with a faint frown, then something made her glance around, to gasp in unwitting delight at what she'd failed to notice in her discomfort. A magnificent basket of flowers sat on her piano.

'Who—you—for me?' she said disjointedly.

'None other,' he replied with some irony.

'But this must have cost you a small fortune! You really shouldn't have. I mean, you really shouldn't be wasting your money like this.'

'Read the card,' he suggested.

Louise stared at him, then walked over to the piano. Her hand hovered over the roses and some intuition warned her that she might need all her composure to deal with this. She swallowed and pulled out the card. It said simply, 'You were magnificent.'

She closed her eyes and said huskily, 'If you think—'

'That I shouldn't thank you for a wonderful day and a thrilling experience, not to mention the rest of it?' he said from right behind her.

She drew a deep breath and turned to face him.

'Or thank you for taking in a lame duck like myself? I'm afraid it's my prerogative, Louise,' he said very quietly, but there was something in his eyes she couldn't decipher. 'Could I be more chivalrous than you thought?'

Her lips parted because suddenly she could see it—a little glint of pure mockery again in his eyes. Then she straightened her shoulders. 'Thank you very much,' she said just as quietly, 'but I still wish you hadn't. Nor, I'm sure, are your motives entirely chivalrous.'

'You could be right,' he said after a long moment and he looked amused. 'But the thing is, you surely don't expect me to simply walk away? There must be something we could say to each other—or there's this, of course.'

'Don't,' she said a little frantically as he put his arms around her.

'You didn't say that last time,' he murmured, and his breath fanned her cheek.

'I was—that was different,' she returned tautly and shivered.

He ran his hands down her arms. 'Not cold, surely? Afraid?' he mused. 'Did I hurt you the last time I kissed you, Louise?'

'No.' She bit her lip and willed herself to break away. But he moved his hands to cup the smooth curves of her shoulders lightly in his palms and a torrent of sensation flowed down her body, taking her breath away and making her feel weak at the knees.

'So?' he said very quietly, and drew her against him. 'We don't have to do it in silence again. There's nothing wrong in saying a thing or two.'

'You wouldn't like what I have in mind to say.' Her lips barely moved but her eyes were scathing.

'How could you? How *dare* you?' he suggested and raised an eyebrow. 'I notice you're not running away.'

'Would you let me?' she challenged. 'Or would you rather I indulged in an undignified little scuffle?'

He smiled slightly but his gaze was curiously heavy as it rested on her lips, then the slim line of her neck down to where it disappeared into the V of her waistcoat.

'I'd much rather we indulged in the sheer pleasure of kissing each other. You were wet then,' he added.

She pressed her lips together firmly.

But he only laughed softly and continued, 'Like a beautiful mermaid. But you kissed me with hunger and passion. You're angry now, although still passionate, I suspect.' He watched the pulse beating rapidly in the silken hollow at the base of her throat, then raised his eyes to hers. 'That could make it even more momentous.'

Louise opened her mouth to protest but was suddenly shaken to the roots of her being as she realized that being angry with this man did not affect the attraction he held for her. If anything, it heightened it, she discovered as she was possessed by the insane desire to kiss him fervently, then turn her back and walk away from him. Her eyes widened and her lips parted in horror.

'A new concept?' Richard Moore hazarded wryly. 'You're not very experienced in these matters, are you, Louise?'

She came to earth with a bump and attempted to wrest herself free. 'That's…that's demeaning!' she panted.

He held her easily. 'No, it's not.' He paused and looked down at her with the corners of his mouth quirking. 'You were the one who didn't think you were soft and cuddly.'

'Let me go!' she said through her teeth.

'In a moment. I'm merely trying to demonstrate that I far prefer your brand of fire, be it willing or be it hostile, to someone who is merely soft and cuddly. Because between two people as attracted to each other as we are the effect can be quite stunning.'

'Look, I *refuse* to play out this tawdry little charade, Mr Moore,' she hissed.

'Oh, it's no charade, Louise,' he drawled. 'Unless you make a habit of enticing strange men into your toils, then discarding them?'

'You make me sound like…like…'

'A black widow spider?' he suggested with a fleeting grin.

That did it. She managed to get one arm free with the express purpose of hitting him, but as she raised it he said with soft insolence, 'Touch a nerve, did I? I wouldn't attempt violence if I were you, Miss Brown. Good girl,' he added as her arm sank and he did kiss her, but very briefly. Then he released her and said, 'Fascinating and mysterious as all this is, we're going to be late. Shall we go to dinner?'

CHAPTER THREE

'THEY'RE not here,' Louise said, five minutes later.

'Have you ever known Neil to be on time?'

'No,' she said tautly and looked around. Once again fairy lights lit the trees and there were candle glasses flickering on the tables. The air was balmy and the fountain on the corner of MacRae Place played its silver jets into a pool of gold.

'Look, sit down.' Richard pulled out a chair at a table for four and after a moment Louise sank down. 'There's no need to look like that,' he added.

'Like what?'

'Pale and haunted.' He paused and frowned. 'Are you all right?'

'Fine!'

He looked as if he was going to take issue with her, then he shrugged and murmured, 'If you say so, Louise.'

She looked away moodily. It being a Monday and a school night, it wasn't as busy, and Louise thought, at least she wouldn't have Amy Lewis to deal with. One saving grace of her day at school had been that she hadn't come in contact with Amy.

However, it proved to be a vain assumption that, because it was a school night, the girl would be at home and studying, because no sooner had Richard sat down than Amy raced over to them excitedly.

'Hi, Miss Brown, Mr Moore! I thought you were leaving soon,' she added to Richard.

'Amy, shouldn't you be home studying?' Louise said with a sigh.

Amy's face fell. 'I know. I'm sorry, Miss Brown, but they rang me and begged me to take the place of one of the girls who's fallen sick. It's only for one night, I promise. You do look nice, Miss Brown,' she added.

'Thank you,' Louise said wearily. 'Uh—my brother is coming for dinner plus another guest.'

'Well, would you like a cocktail to start with? The house speciality is a delicious combination of pineapple juice, Cointreau and cream,' Amy said importantly, addressing her words to Richard.

'Two of those sound just the thing, Amy,' he replied, giving her the full benefit of his lazy smile.

Causing Louise to say, as Amy drifted away on cloud nine, 'You shouldn't.'

'You don't seriously believe I'm trying to attach an eighteen-year-old kid, Louise?' he retorted.

She bit her lip and was startled to discover that her nerves were jangling almost to screaming pitch. Calm down, she told herself. But how to?

'There you are!' another voice said, and Neil was standing before them.

Richard rose and the girl beside Neil threw her arms around him. 'I've had a lovely, lovely afternoon, Richard. Birds, birds and more birds... You must be Neil's sister.' She turned to Louise. 'Hi! I'm Eve Parker. Neil's told me so much about you.'

Louise made an effort to collect herself and looked briefly past this eager girl into her brother's eyes—to get another shock as she disturbed a nervous but intense little look in them. He's serious at last, she thought shakily. He wants my approval...

'Hello!' She extended her hand to Eve and smiled warmly. 'Uh—Richard's told me a bit about *you*. Do sit down. Uh…'

But she didn't have to search for any more to say because Eve plonked herself into a chair, fanned herself energetically with her hand and gushed into speech. 'Isn't it hot? Sit down, Neil. I agree with you, by the way; your sister is gorgeous! But you're not much alike—which doesn't mean to say you aren't gorgeous too, darling! I didn't mean that. You mustn't mind me Louise,' she confided. 'I'm famous for speaking my mind.'

'As I'm beginning to discover,' Neil said ruefully, then turned. 'Why, Amy, we'll have two of those, thank you. Then the menu.'

'Right away, Mr Brown,' Amy said pertly, and set a brimming glass with a gay little paper parasol in front of Louise. 'I made them myself,' she said tenderly to Louise, then glanced provocatively at Richard from under her lashes as she set his down before she bustled away.

'I told you so,' Louise murmured, with a scathing look at Richard.

'Told you so—what?' Neil asked.

Louise set her teeth and wished devoutly for a cyclone to demolish MacRae Place. Richard, on the other hand, smiled charmingly and said, 'We were in the middle of a slight domestic, that's all.'

'I thought you two had only just met,' Eve remarked as Neil's startled gaze dwelt on his sister.

Louise drew a very deep breath and the oxygen, or the adrenalin—one of the two—gave her the spirit to change tack brilliantly. 'I'm dying to know how you and Neil met,' she said enthusiastically to Eve.

Eve needed no second invitation to explain that she and Neil had literally bumped into each other, knocking each other over on a crowded Melbourne street six months ago, and had kept in touch ever since. It was at Eve's invitation, in fact, that Neil had gone haring off to East Gippsland to do some bird-watching.

'But he didn't...' Louise stopped awkwardly, flashed a confused look at her brother, opened her mouth but had the words taken right out of it.

'Didn't tell you about me?' Eve said. 'Don't be offended, Louise. We decided to tell no one until we were really sure we had something to tell. Didn't we, darling?' she said to Neil.

Louise stared at her brother with her mouth open.

Neil looked momentarily as if he, too, wished MacRae Place might disappear but he took the plunge and said bravely, 'Yes, Lou, we did. The thing is, we decided only a couple of days ago to, well, get married after Christmas. I was going to tell you before that, of course, but what with forgetting about Richard and having to dash back, et cetera, it all—' he looked as helpless and bothered as only Neil could '—got a bit tangled up.'

'Well.' Louise cleared her throat. 'Well, *congratulations*,' she said. 'I can't pretend I'm not absolutely stunned but—well, it's come so out of the blue.'

'Of course!' Eve nodded understandingly, then looked impish. 'Now you don't have to say another word until you get to know me better.' And she reached over to pat Louise's hand. At the same time she took up the reins of the evening and before long they were chatting as any group of four might do over dinner.

The cocktails were downed and once she felt serene again Louise took the time to study the other girl. Eve Parker was slightly overweight but tall enough to carry it with aplomb. Nothing about her stood out; she had plain brown hair and plain features, although good skin and merry brown eyes.

Her hands were surprisingly slim and elegant, and her teeth were very white, but her clothes were nondescript and baggy—a shapeless white blouse over a batik long skirt that looked distinctly washed out. But the force of her personality was another matter altogether. It was obvious that Neil was extremely taken with this girl. So that's what he was looking for, Louise thought with some bemusement and then found herself thinking, Lucky him, as she watched them laughing together.

A moment later, as they tucked into the house's famous lasagne, her thoughts were brutally drawn back to Richard Moore.

'So, Richard,' Neil said, 'how's fame and fortune treating you? Well, fame anyway. I don't think fortune was ever a problem, you lucky dog.'

'It certainly was not.' Eve helped herself to salad. 'My papa always says the Moore family is a money-printing machine in its own right.'

Louise choked on a mouthful of lasagne and Eve offered to bang her on the back, whilst Neil concernedly topped up her wine glass and advised her to have a sip.

'No, thanks, I'm fine,' she said huskily with her eyes watering. 'I will be.'

'Yes,' Eve continued, 'we Parkers, good as toilet paper and tissues have been to us, can't really hold a candle to you Moores. It irks my papa, I have to tell you, Richard,' she confessed. 'I can remember saying to him once, What is it about the Moore family that bugs you so? Do you know what he answered?' She laughed mischievously and looked teasingly at Richard.

'No.'

'He said, ''I can go around in my Roller, fly around in my jet, your mother can be literally dripping in diamonds, but if there's a Moore within a mile I might as well not exist.'''

'My apologies,' Richard said wryly.

'Oh, don't apologize to me!' Eve waved an airy hand. 'One thing I didn't inherit from Papa was the desire to impress the world. Louise, are you sure you're all right? You look a little pale.'

'This is all news to Louise, I'm afraid,' Richard said, and added regretfully, 'She assumed I was one of your lame ducks, Neil.'

Neil stared, gasped, then started to laugh. 'But Lou, surely you recognized the name? I mean, Richard's famous in his own right apart from his family. His wildlife documentaries and photojournalism are stunning! He's done more to bring the plight of the African rhino and elephant to the world's notice than anyone I know.'

Everything fell into place for Louise at once. She remembered a couple of remarks that hadn't made sense that very morning. She vividly remembered standing in her bedroom the day Richard had arrived with something pricking her consciousness. She remembered thinking that something didn't quite gel about him, that there seemed to be more to him than just a loner and a misfit. Why, oh, why didn't I listen to myself? she asked herself despairingly. On the other hand, she thought abruptly, why didn't he *tell* me?

She said slowly, not looking at him, 'I'm afraid I've

yet to work out what kind of game your Richard is playing, Neil. I may have been remiss in not recognizing the
name but *he* actively chose to mislead me.'

'I wouldn't call it actively,' Richard drawled.

'Oh, no?' Louise turned to him at last. 'How about
the gem to do with photography being a hard field to
break into? How about—' she paused and searched her
mind '—the mention of having to wander the *streets* if
I didn't put you up for the night? How about that—
that—' she all but choked again '—pearl of the first
water to do with not being *quite* broke?'

'Ah, that one crept in, I'm afraid, when you were
about to insist on paying for your own coffee, as if you'd
decided I was absolutely penniless,' he said mildly, although with an ironic little glint of his teeth. 'As for
photography, it is a hard field to break into; I didn't
actually tell a lie there—'

But Louise had had enough. She threw her napkin
onto the table and stood up. 'Excuse me,' she said
coldly, 'but I can't stand people who play with words,
or the truth.'

'But, Lou—' Neil stood up agitatedly '—I'm sure we
can sort this out. Blame *me*, why don't you? It really is
all my fault.'

'No, it is not, but I'll tell you something, Neil. Either
he goes or I do. In the meantime I'm going for a walk.'
She swept away, all but knocking over Amy, who was
clearing the next table.

'Let her go,' she heard Eve advising Neil softly.
'Sometimes you need to be on your own to adjust to
things. I'm sure she'll calm down in a while.'

That's all I need, Louise thought irrationally. Some

strange woman deciding how I should be handled and advising my own brother on the matter!

She strode up the Avenue towards the beach and, when she got there, slipped her sandals off and set off briskly towards the Spit. She'd only gone a few yards when Richard stepped into place beside her.

'Go away,' she ordered.

'No.'

She stopped and swung to confront him with her hands on her hips. 'I meant every word of it, Mr Moore. It's you or me.' Her green eyes were furious.

'Why are you so angry, Louise?'

'You don't think I have any right to be?' she marvelled. 'If nothing else, you had to know the truth was likely to come out tonight, thereby making me look an absolute *fool*.'

'Perhaps,' he conceded. 'But I did offer to tell you more about me this afternoon.'

'Oh, yes, I remember!' she mocked. 'You don't think that was a little belated? Strangely enough, I do!' She dropped her hands and started to walk again.

'And *you* don't think misjudging me fairly comprehensively brought on this excess of rage?' he suggested dryly after a moment.

'I didn't misjudge you in the slightest,' she said through her teeth. 'I was always suspicious of you, with, it is now revealed, good cause!'

'Even when you were in my arms?'

She paused, then said tautly, 'I've told you what I thought about that.'

They eyed each other.

'Based,' he suggested with gentle satire, 'on my complete lack of—shall we say—prospects, Louise? As you thought then.'

'Based,' she said, 'if you must know, Richard Moore, on a desire not to compound what had to be a moment of madness.'

'Only a moment, Louise?'

'Look.' Her shoulders slumped suddenly. 'All right, I don't know what possessed me. I barely know you. I'm appalled, if you must know, to think I could have... Whether you're a lame duck or the richest man in the world makes no difference to how I feel about myself.'

He said nothing for a long moment as the surf crashed rhythmically behind them.

Time enough for Louise to gather herself together. She squared her shoulders resolutely and looked at him proudly. 'So, while I may have been less than wise, you needn't think it absolves you—'

'I never considered the matter in the light of either of us needing absolution,' he broke in swiftly.

'Ah. But say Neil *hadn't* remembered and come rushing back. What had you planned to do in that event, Richard? Lead me on even *further* until you'd had enough, only to disappear so that I mightn't find out who you were until you'd gone? Is that *really* why you persisted with my original mistake?'

'What do you mean?' He frowned at her.

She put her head to one side. 'It's just occurred to me that it might have been a very handy thing to have happened. For a man who had no intention of developing more than a—shall we say—' her eyes mocked him '—a brief *fling*.'

'If you're piqued because I didn't make up my mind

to win you and wed you the moment I laid eyes on you, Louise—'

'Oh, go to hell!' she snapped, and started to walk fast. 'You know very well what I mean,' she called over her shoulder, and broke into a run.

He caught her and she tried to free herself but to no avail, getting the bottom of her skirt wet as the surf lapped around their feet. Then she dropped her sandals and as they both scrabbled to retrieve them a rogue wave sneaked up on them, knocking Louise off her feet and drenching Richard up to the knees.

'Look, enough,' he said as she sat up gasping and spluttering. 'I've got them.'

'I'm soaked!' she groaned. 'I'm—'

'You'll be soaked again soon. You carry your shoes, I'll carry you. Up you come.'

'Oh, no, you don't!' She leapt up and beat a hasty retreat. But once out of reach of the surf she doubled up suddenly with a stitch.

He came up beside her. 'Have a breather, at least, Louise.'

She straightened and would have given all she possessed to be able to stalk away with dignity. But her breathing was erratic, her hair was sopping and hanging in her eyes, her clothes were dripping.

She cast her eyes heavenwards suddenly, scraped back her hair and said intensely, 'I could kill you! On top of everything else you've made me a laughing stock in front of one of my own students—I really could kill you, Richard Moore!'

'Before you do that, why don't you sit down?' he replied equably. 'You could have my shirt. Why don't you take your skirt off at least?' He unbuttoned his shirt, shrugged out of it and handed it to her.

'Now that is such a practical suggestion,' she taunted. 'Am I supposed to walk home wearing your shirt? You don't think I'd feel a little odd?'

'Very odd,' he agreed. 'But if you took your skirt and top off, putting my shirt on for the time being, we could at least wring your clothes out so that when we do walk home you won't look quite so all-but-drowned. There's no one around,' he added after a brief scan of the beach.

Louise looked downwards and gritted her teeth. 'Turn your back,' she commanded.

He did, but only after a clashing little exchange of glances.

She scrambled awkwardly out of her top and skirt and pulled his shirt on, buttoning it up as quickly as she could.

'Ready?' he asked.

'As ready as I'll ever be,' she muttered, picking up her skirt and proceeding to wring the life out of it. He picked up her top and dealt with it more gently. 'Look, there's a patch of grass up there,' he commented. 'Let's lay them out on it.'

'I'm not intending to spend much time here. With you. Like this,' she warned.

He didn't respond but carried her clothes to where there was some long, spiky grass pushing through the sand on top of a dune and laid them out neatly, stretching them to smooth the wrinkles.

Louise watched this exercise cynically for a moment, then she sank down on the dune, clasping her arms about her knees. Only to discover, unfortunately, that his shirt was a heady reminder of being in his arms. Its cotton was still warm from his body and carried a clean, pure man tang. She stared down the beach, watching the silver tracery of the phosphorus in the surf that the moonlight picked out, as well as the long, lazy swell of the deep waters beyond the breakers.

It occurred to her that what she was going through at the moment was not unlike being all at sea in those depths—a thought that didn't improve her disposition at all.

He came to sit beside her. 'At least it's not cold,' he observed mildly.

She glanced at him and was not at all surprised that of the two of them she not only felt the sillier but probably looked it too with her soaked hair, huddling into a man's shirt. He, on the other hand, just looked magnificent with his broad golden shoulders and sleek torso disappearing into his new khaki trousers. 'The weather!' she said witheringly. 'How lucky we are to have that to fall back on.'

He chuckled. 'OK. You choose a topic. I had the feeling you might welcome a change of subject, that's all.'

Louise laid her cheek on her knees. 'If anyone needs a change of topic, it's you,' she contradicted him. 'To get away from the subject of brief flings if nothing else.'

'Look,' he said evenly after a moment, 'I had no intention of—letting things get out of hand, either. If we agree to disagree about everything else, I think we should concede that it was something quite spontaneous. If we're to be honest.'

'Because you're Richard Moore? Scion of the mighty Moore family, not to mention famed photojournalist and documentary maker?' Louise said slowly, resting her chin on her knees this time. 'Is that why you had no intention of letting things get out of hand, or so you say? I mean, is it a problem when girls or women know who you are? Do you have to fend them off?'

'I wouldn't say that exactly—'

'Look, Richard—' She glanced at him sardonically. 'Put yourself in my place,' she invited. 'Forgive me for saying so but you did wangle yourself in in the first place. You did—there was—all *right*, there was something spontaneous between us but there also had to be some good reason not to tell me who you were. I may have acted rashly but I'm not a complete fool.'

'You—' his lips twisted and he shrugged ruefully '—were so convinced I was a lame duck I'm afraid I—reacted to it. I'm sorry. I shouldn't have done it.'

'You even managed to look the part—may I say in my defence?' she retaliated.

'You tend to look a bit ragged at the edges after a flight from Africa. It took me nearly twenty-four hours to fly from Dar es Salaam to the Gold Coast with a few stops thrown in. I'd also spent a month in the Serengeti, which can be hard on your clothes.'

Louise digested this but refused to allow a glimmer of interest or sympathy to show. 'And?'

He raised an eyebrow at her.

'If I'd known who you were despite your less than sartorial appearance, what then?'

He didn't reply immediately. Then he said dryly, almost bleakly, it seemed, 'Who knows?'

'So we're not much further forward, are we?' she mused barely audibly.

He glanced at her narrowly but she was scooping little handfuls of sand, then watching it trickle through her fingers. 'We're—calmer about it, at least,' he said wryly. 'Neil is devastated.'

Louise framed an extremely uncomplimentary comment on the subject of her brother but left it unsaid at the last moment. Instead she said, 'She—I'm still reeling about *that*. She...' She stopped helplessly.

'It could be what he needs.'

'You know her well?'

'I'd never met her. Although I'd heard of the family.'

'She greeted you like a long-lost friend,' Louise murmured.

'I think she's one of those demonstrative people, that's all.'

Louise straightened. 'Well, I'm not backing down, Richard.'

He was silent for a moment, then asked, 'Because of a loss of face in front of Eve Parker?'

Louise bit her lip.

'It wouldn't do to get a complex about her, you know.'

She cast him a speaking look. 'You must think I'm crazy—because I'm suffering from a complex about *you*,' she said bitterly. 'I'd really rather not have to face you every time I turn around. Whatever the rights and wrongs of it are—' she raised her hands warningly '—I reserve *that* right.'

'I wouldn't go far, you know,' he said after a moment's thought.

'What do you mean?' She looked at him sharply.

He returned her look with a wicked little glint in his eyes. 'I'd go to a hotel, that's all. I still aim to spend the fortnight with Neil, doing what he's set his heart on doing.'

'That's...that's blackmail,' she said heatedly.

'Not really,' he drawled. 'It's simply an offer to move to a hotel.'

Louise made a disgusted sound. 'Why are you persisting with this?'

'In the hope that I might be able to redeem myself slightly?'

'Are you asking me or telling me?' she said moodily.

His lips twisted. 'Asking you. Is it at all possible, do you think?'

'I'll tell you what I think,' she said slowly. 'I don't believe in brief flings, Richard Moore. So if you're hoping to pursue that line, think again.'

She stood up abruptly and walked over to her skirt and top. They were still wet but she put them on quickly and handed him back his shirt. 'Home, James,' she said briefly. 'I've had enough for one night.'

'Whatever you say, Louise. But I can stay?'

She glanced at him ironically. 'Just don't try anything, Mr Moore.'

She was positively regal as they walked home, past the café, where there was no sign of Neil and Eve and where not only Amy but a few other diners raised eyebrows at her damp and sandy appearance. She ignored it all with her head held high and her shoulders back.

Which caused Richard to say with a wry little smile, as they let themselves into the town house. 'Another masterly performance, Louise.'

She looked at him through the fringe of her lashes but said only, 'I'm going to bed. Goodnight.'

He seemed about to say something, then murmured, 'Goodnight. Sleep well.'

She started up the staircase, conscious that he was watching her and conscious as well of the strange, magnetic pull of his gaze on her back. No, she said to herself. Oh, no. I know what you're thinking but the answer is no.

All the same, it took more courage than she'd bargained for to shut herself into her bedroom, more willpower to ignore a curiously weak-kneed sensation than she'd dreamt could be the case. Because to think of Richard Moore downstairs on his own was suddenly almost more than she could bear as she remembered the feel of his mouth on hers, his fingers in her hair, his hard, strong body against hers.

The shower she took sluiced away the salt and sand, then she put on a pair of blue lawn short pyjamas trimmed with satin ribbon and dried her hair. She paused to study the faint blue shadows under her eyes and the slight pallor of her skin, considering that despite what anyone else might think they were actually welcome. Because the cause of them was also the cause of enormous relief—she wasn't pregnant.

She didn't hear the phone ring about an hour later, having fallen deeply asleep.

Richard did, rousing himself from a brown study, and he took the call on the lounge extension. It was Neil.

'She's fine,' Richard said in answer to the query that was full of brotherly concern. 'She's asleep.' He paused. 'Look, mate, you obviously have some idea of what happened... Yes, I did rather ladle on the lame duck impression, I'm afraid... No, I...' He paused again, then said abruptly, 'I've tried to apologize but—' He broke off and hardly managed to get a word in edgeways for the next five minutes.

Because Neil Brown took the opportunity to deliver a tribute to his sister at the same time as he, not so subtly, indicated just how right she could be for Richard.

'She's never happier than when she's helping people, which would fit in with your work admirably,' he said. 'She's compulsive,' he added. 'It worries me at times because I keep expecting someone to take advantage of her. I'm only surprised, if she thought you were a lame duck, that she didn't fix you up with a job. She always worries dreadfully about the rest of them.'

And then he delivered the gem of an idea. 'You could be so right for her,' he said. 'She's such a warm, lovely person and I'm sure all that do-good zeal would, well, settle down a bit if it was channelled into a relationship with a real man. And if there is a spark between you two, and Eve's sure there must be, don't let this spoil it. She'll come round!'

'And you obviously didn't divine the whole story,' Richard murmured aloud, after finally putting the phone down, and smiled faintly at the thought of Louise's reception of her brother's summing-up of her. But the smile faded almost as soon as it was born. I wonder if Eve did divine more of the story, on the other hand? he pondered. I've got the feeling you're particularly perceptive, Eve Parker. Why do I get the feeling there's more to this than meets the eye?

He frowned but nothing presented itself to him by way of explanation and presently he found himself thinking about the night on the boat. But the memories that came made him swear beneath his breath and get up to roam around the room restlessly.

*   *   *

Louise woke up at two o'clock in the morning to discover that she was starving. She tossed and turned for a few minutes, then gave in and got up.

The house was in darkness and she moved through it quietly and shut herself into the kitchen before putting on the light, only to come to grief immediately. She turned back from the light switch to trip over a basket that should have been on the counter but was on the floor, bumped into the adjacent counter and knocked over a tin of coffee. It bounced noisily several times before the lid fell off and coffee showered everywhere.

She held her breath but the fates were obviously against her, she decided as a door down the hall opened. Then the kitchen door opened cautiously and Richard stood there.

All he wore was a T-shirt and a pair of boxer shorts, and he blinked owlishly against the light and ran his hand through his hair before saying, 'Thought you were a burglar.'

'No, as you see. I'm only surprised I didn't wake Neil.' She opened a cupboard and took out a dustpan. 'This hasn't been my day.'

'Neil isn't here,' he said, and came over to help her.

'Oh. How do you know?'

'He rang about an hour after you'd gone to bed. He was worried about you. He also mentioned that he—might not come home tonight.'

'Couldn't have been too worried.' Louise got down on her knees and started sweeping up coffee.

'I think he feels you're quite safe with me.'

'Little does he know.'

'Louise, let me,' Richard said firmly, and took the

brush and dustpan out of her hands. 'Sit down. You wouldn't have been hungry, would you?'

She blinked but the close proximity, for they were both on their knees only inches apart, got the better of her. She rose and walked over to the kitchen table. 'How did you know?'

'You had about two mouthfuls of your dinner. As a matter of fact, I only had three. What say I make up some toasted sandwiches?'

She sat down and rubbed her face. 'All right.'

He did it with such little fuss, she was moved to remark on it when he placed two golden ham and cheese sandwiches in front of her and poured her a cup of tea. 'For a Moore, let alone a man, you're amazing. How did you become so expert?'

He sat opposite and smiled modestly. 'When you spend a lot of time on safari you pick up all sorts of skills.'

'Ah, yes.' She paused and frowned. 'I don't know a great deal about the Moore family but aren't they heavily into banking, high finance and the like?'

'Some of us are. My father is but the Moore fortune was all based on sheep originally.'

'And what does your father think of you not following in his footsteps?'

'It annoys him immensely. But then everything about me annoys my father.'

Louise looked at him with more interest. 'A clash of personalities?'

'You could say so. My older brother is much more to his liking, probably because he did tread the ordained path.'

'What about your mother?'

'She tends to approve of anyone who opposes my father. They have what you might call an "open" marriage. They loathe each other ninety per cent of the time.'

Louise picked up her cup. 'How—uncomfortable. Did they never consider parting?'

'Many times, I'm sure. It would be a little difficult to sort out the financial side of things, particularly as she keeps threatening to take him for every penny he's got were he to discard her. My father,' he said dryly, 'and his money are not easily parted.'

'And this career of yours...' Louise studied him intently. 'Would you say you deliberately went out to do something your father would take exception to?'

'How perceptive of you, Louise.' He looked at her amusedly. 'No, I didn't, although I did vow I'd—' he raised an eyebrow '—make my *own* name. But I was always fascinated by photography and film-making. When I said I wasn't a nine-to-five man, that was true. I loathe banking and finance. As a matter of fact, I loathe law although I tried that to please father. But in the end I couldn't hack it.'

'So you're a lawyer?'

'I have a law degree; put it that way. Does it make me more acceptable?' he asked with that wicked little glint. 'I have to tell you I'll never practise it.'

Louise sat back and finished her sandwiches in silence.

'Sorry,' he said after a while. 'I've offended you.'

She took her time and poured herself another cup of tea before she answered. 'I wonder what you would have done if I'd fallen into your arms as soon as I heard you were a Moore?' she said reflectively. 'One of *those* Moores, albeit a black sheep one.'

He grimaced. 'Point taken, Miss Brown. No, I can't accuse you of that. In fact, that's a point I've been trying to make, with little success. How you fell into my arms was a simple coming together of two people who were magnificently matched whatever their backgrounds.' He shrugged. 'Which is, to my mind, more important than anything else.'

Louise stood up. 'I'm sure,' she said scornfully. 'I'm going back to bed.' She pulled the edges of her blue robe together and tightened her sash. 'Thanks for supper.'

But he was on his feet in a flash and he put a hand on her arm to detain her. 'No, you don't,' he said roughly. 'I've had enough of this. You—'

'Let me go,' she warned through her teeth. 'How despicable—'

'What do you think I'm going to do?' he shot back. 'Rape you while your brother's out of the house? Forget it, Louise—'

'I refuse to discuss this!'

'Because you think that will make it go away?' His eyes were very blue and scornful. 'Well, it so happens there's one thing *I* refuse to do any longer and that's gloss over or skirt around what happened. We *slept* together, Louise. Apart from anything else, and heaven alone knows why you're refusing to discuss even this with me, that's how women get pregnant.'

CHAPTER FOUR

'I'M NOT,' she whispered.

'How can you know?' Richard demanded. 'Have you had a test?'

Louise swallowed and looked away. 'No.'

He paused, then his eyes narrowed as they lingered on the shadows beneath her eyes. 'Oh,' he said. 'So that's why you were looking pale?'

She nodded briefly.

'Well, if that's not driving you out of your mind with anxiety, which I could have understood only too well, why are you so determined to…act as if it never happened?'

Louise didn't answer and his gaze became hard and intent again.

'It's not as if we didn't do it joyfully with no questions asked, no apologies. And you fell asleep in my arms afterwards as if you trusted me implicitly and slept all night through,' he added brutally.

Louise breathed erratically and her breasts lifted the blue lawn.

He noted it and a nerve flickered in his jaw before he went on deliberately, 'It was magnificent, you were magnificent, there were no holds barred and it wasn't simply sex, it was an expression of our admiration for each other. It happened, Louise, marvellously, because you're not only beautiful but brave and there was no way *we* could help ourselves.' He paused and stared into her wide green eyes. 'Can you deny any of that?'

'I...' she said barely audibly, unable to remain unmoved at the echo of her own thoughts as well as the memories he'd evoked. A tremor ran down her body. 'No.'

He watched her like a hawk. 'Look, sit down again and let's talk about it rationally for once.'

She hesitated, running her hands up her arms, then did as she was bid.

'Perhaps you'd like to start the ball rolling by telling me what you're going through,' he suggested. 'Hang on, though.' He left the kitchen and came back moments later with a bottle of cognac and two liqueur glasses.

Louise thought of objecting but decided she needed some medicinal support if nothing else. 'I...' She toyed with her glass and stared into the amber depths. 'I never believed it could happen that way, if you must know,' she said at last. 'I was always firmly of the opinion you *should* be able to help yourself.'

'If it's any consolation, so was I.'

She looked up and was amazed to see he was deadly serious.

'Go on,' he said quietly.

She shrugged and sipped some of the fiery liquid. 'How do *you* feel when you've been—caught out being all moral and superior only to find you have feet of clay?'

He smiled faintly. 'Foolish.'

'Yes, well,' she said with some irony, then sighed. 'But what worries me more is I believed, I did honestly believe, you had to be in love with someone to...for...if you know what I mean.'

'Have you ever been in love?'

'I thought so, once. It didn't last.'

'You mistook lust for love?' he suggested. 'If so, you wouldn't be the first, Louise. Was he the one who indicated you weren't soft and cuddly enough?'

She coloured faintly and said unsteadily, 'Yes—well—but I'm not so sure if it was either love *or* lust. I—' she licked her lips '—sometimes wonder whether I didn't persuade myself I *should* be in love because it seemed to be happening to everyone I knew. And I thought I could help him with his career—he was a historian—but I sort of got the feeling, eventually, that I would be the meal ticket while he stayed home to write obscure theses.' She gestured helplessly.

'Louise.' Richard stared at her. 'No wonder Neil—' He stopped abruptly. 'Go on.'

'Well—' she blinked '—this is all in hindsight, of course. Because when it fell apart I was left wondering how I could have been so wrong, about myself and about him.'

'So the sex wasn't—up to much?' He raised a quizzical eyebrow at her.

'Why do men always have sex on the brain?' she returned acidly.

He grinned fleetingly. 'I was just trying to sort out what you fell for in this man. If there wasn't much physical desire involved—now that was asking for trouble, Louise.'

'There was. I'm not a complete idiot,' she retorted. 'It just...' She shrugged and sighed.

'Never really came up to expectations, for which he laid the blame at your door? You couldn't have proved him more wrong the other night,' he said dryly.

Louise would have given anything at that moment to be able to evade his slightly amused but so penetrating gaze. She finished her cognac, coughed slightly, then said with her eyes watering, 'Which makes it even more inexplicable that I should have done what I did.'

'We did.'

'OK, *we* did.' She looked at him feeling somewhat goaded. 'So. Tell me your thoughts on the matter now.'

He sat back and stretched his legs out. 'One thing before I do. I'm not sure that what happened to us is any worse than believing you're in love, when what you really want is to be a guardian angel.'

'I didn't think that at the time,' she said through her teeth. 'I mean, I thought it was something we would have in common. Don't—'

'Let me finish.' He looked amused again. 'I'm not saying either is particularly wrong, just human nature. What I'm trying to say is, don't castigate yourself too much. After all, what you thought was love as well as a common cause let you down—if you see what I mean.'

She stared at him and shook her head. 'Won't work, Mr Moore. Nothing is going to make me feel—good about succumbing to a one-night stand with a man I barely knew. And if you suggest it needn't *be* a one-night stand at this point in time I could—bite.'

He laughed. 'Sorry.'

'Why don't you return the compliment? You said a little while ago that you hadn't believed you could lose control like that—so? I mean, can you honestly tell me that bringing Louise Brown down a peg or two, which you've admitted was your motivation for not telling me who you were, didn't include just a teeny bit of seduction?'

He sat forward, toyed with his glass and drained it abruptly. 'I can tell you this. From the moment I laid eyes on you I was aware that you were gorgeous, but who wouldn't be? Then there was a certain imperiousness about you, when you weren't as wary as hell—'

'You don't think I had a right to be wary, if nothing else?'

'Wary, yes.' His lips twisted. 'But it was more than that—to be honest, I first wondered what it would be like to make love to you when you stalked up the stairs as if it was all my fault that your robe was virtually see-through.'

'I didn't!'

'Oh, yes, you did...'

She opened her mouth but nothing intelligible came out.

'Believe me,' he murmured. 'But all through those two days, while I was thinking of you like that, just as you were starting to wonder about me, I had no intention of actually—achieving it.' He looked at her with a tinge of irritation.

'How kind of you, but—' she paused and frowned suddenly '—why?' The query seemed to linger on the air.

'You were the sister of a friend,' he said after a moment. 'You, it became patently obvious, weren't that kind of girl.'

'And not the kind of girl,' she said slowly, 'it might have seemed worthwhile to get to know better?'

Their gazes locked. 'There's hardly been time to do that, Louise.'

She thought for a bit, then said on a breath, 'Can I tell you something? You've accused me of despising myself for sleeping with you because I thought you were beneath me. But while a lot of things didn't make sense and while I certainly may have, in my ignorance, wished there was a bit more substance to you, the one enduring impression I had still abides, even now I know just how much substance there is to you.'

She paused and looked at him steadily. 'I thought then and I still think that you're a loner at heart, Richard. Am I right?'

It was a critical little silence that ensued. He looked briefly surprised, as if he was examining something far off, then his gaze focused. 'I…' he said at last. 'No, I can't deny the charge.'

'Then can you understand why, when I woke up the next morning, I was suddenly besieged by very grave reservations, to put it mildly? I don't know what it's like for men but—' She put a hand to her mouth, then forced herself to finish. 'It's not something I ever thought I could do, especially when I knew there probably wasn't any future for us.'

'Louise—so how do you account for it?'

She stood up. 'I can't,' she said wearily. 'You're right. What happened doesn't seem susceptible to any kind of accounting. And that's why I think we should just leave it at that. Especially since I'm not pregnant.'

'Do you at least acquit me of deliberate seduction?'

She looked at him broodingly. 'Do you have any idea what it's like to remember—' she opened her hands futilely '—offering to get you a job on a fashion magazine? Offering to talk Neil into taking you to Africa?'

He moved restlessly and said sombrely, 'Yes.'

'And then,' she said quietly, 'I think there is the problem of you being Richard Moore. I'm sure you're the target of a lot of female admiration so that, even if only subconsciously, you're— Talk about being wary! Can you tell me you're not?'

'Yes, I can,' he said with a slight smile. 'I know I feature as the villain in all this, Louise, but I'm old enough not to get trapped by a lot of female admiration.'

She shrugged. 'Anyway, my premise still stands. The fact that you wanted no real involvement was probably the underlying reason for all my doubts, but now you know you don't have to worry.'

'Strangely enough I still do,' he said with irony.

'Well, you don't *have* to so there's nothing to keep you here, is there?' she said with some impatience. 'Unless you seriously intend to pursue jabiru with Neil and Eve? I don't understand how someone as famous as you got trapped into this in the first place,' she added bitterly. 'It has to be a bit of a come-down from elephants and rhino! I don't even know if the jabiru is endangered except, perhaps, in this small corner of the world.'

'I'm beginning to wonder about that myself.' He stared at nothing with a frown in his eyes.

'What do you mean?'

He brought his gaze back to her, then shrugged. 'Neil and I *have* known each other on and off for a couple of years. We did meet at Dubbo originally and we spent a bit of time together at the Lapalala Game Reserve in South Africa, where they specialize in rhino conservation as well as having a wilderness school, but—' He stopped and frowned.

'All this is very interesting—but what?'

'Then we bumped into each other at a conference a couple of months ago and—up came this invitation. It took me a bit by surprise, but Neil was quite insistent and he painted a very pleasant picture of lazing about on the Broadwater, so I agreed. I knew I'd be due for a break and he's good company, we have a lot in common, but...' He paused.

'Go on.'

'I can't work out why he didn't tell me about you, that's all. Or tell you about me for that matter.'

Louise gestured. 'You know Neil.'

'Yes, but I mightn't have come if...' This time he stopped completely and for the first time since she'd met him Richard Moore looked slightly discomfited, Louise thought. Her mind raced suddenly.

'If you'd known he had an unmarried sister?' she said. 'That's what you were going to say, isn't it. Of all the arrogance...' She stopped, gasped, then breathed, 'No. No, Neil is not like that! Are you trying to say he *planned* to bring us together? He wouldn't have given the matter that much thought. And he isn't conniving in the slightest!'

'No?' Richard eyed her. 'He himself told me only a couple of hours ago to hang in there because he thinks you need a real man and I just might be it.'

Louise blinked, then put a hand to her brow. 'You mean,' she said unsteadily, 'that Neil Brown, my own brother, got you here on false pretences? Deliberately didn't mention he had an unmarried sister, which he knew might put you off, because he hoped we might— we might—get involved?'

'I'm afraid so. It's just hit me but it's the only thing that seems to make sense.'

Louise sat down abruptly. 'I...I... Does that mean he's worried about me because I haven't got a man?' she said dazedly.

'It—' Richard grimaced '—well, that he's worried about you falling for the wrong man—as obviously happened in the past.'

What she said then brought a smile to his lips. 'But why?' she asked helplessly. 'I had no idea! I was worried about *him*, and how on earth *he* was ever going to find someone to spend his life with. This is crazy!'

'It has its humorous side,' he agreed.

'Humorous! But what made him worry about me like that? There's no one I'm interested in—there's no one,' she finished frustratedly.

'It might have been something quite different. In the generous shape of Eve Parker.' His lips twisted. 'Just say he was aware of how stuck on the girl he was even *then*, when he and I last met. If so, he could have already been worried about you being left alone and prey to…being taken advantage of again.'

Louise's mouth fell open. 'Look,' she said feebly. 'Just because it happened once—oh, this is impossible!'

'I don't think it is. It's a fine example of brotherly love, if you ask me,' Richard said quizzically.

'Then tell me this—what made him choose *you*?' she eyed him tauntingly.

'He must have thought we would suit. He was right about that in certain respects,' he replied with a direct little look.

Louise rubbed her face. 'This has got me absolutely floored,' she confessed.

'It's also got us off the real point.'

She blinked at him.

'Our extremely passionate encounter, if you'll forgive me for saying so,' he murmured.

'Oh, that,' she said briefly and wrinkled her brow to concentrate elsewhere.

His expression defied description for a moment, then he started to laugh softly.

'You think this is all funny?'

'I think you're—amazing, Louise,' he said wryly. 'I think whoever does marry you will have to undertake certain exercises to keep your mind on him.'

'Such as?' she said ominously.

'Daily sex?' he suggested. 'You've certainly managed to put us on a back burner, and our encounter was probably as good as it comes, as well as only having happened about thirty hours ago.'

'I *hate* talking about it like that.'

'And I'm beginning to wonder whether it came as such a revelation to you that you have no idea how to handle it, other than by trying to pretend it never happened,' he mused.

If you only knew, crossed Louise's mind, but she immediately hid this treacherous thought by veiling her eyes from him and glancing at her watch. 'Oh, no!' she said immediately. 'It's three o'clock.'

'See what I mean?' he said softly and wickedly.

'Actually, all there is to see,' she retorted, 'is that I have to go to work in a few short hours and I'm not only exhausted, I feel as if I've been through a wringer!'

'Now that—' he smiled faintly and stood up '—is another matter. Up you come.'

She stared at the hand he was holding down to her and noticed it had fine freckles on the back as well as being square and powerful. She raised her eyes and they were uncertain. 'Come where?'

'To bed. Your own bed, on your own.'

'I...'

But he took her hand and pulled her up gently. 'What time do you have to leave here at the latest?'

She looked confused, then made an effort to concentrate. 'Um—I have a free first period so nine o'clock. Why?'

'I'll wake you in time to leave here by nine, that's all. Just go to bed and go to sleep and leave the rest to me.'

'Are you serious?' She looked into his eyes and saw that familiar glint of amusement in their depths.

'Perfectly. But one last thing.' He put his arms around her loosely and looked down at her quite seriously this time. 'You asked me why I'm staying on in the teeth of such furious opposition from you, not to mention my own possible shortcomings. I'm doing it,' he said quietly, 'because it's struck me that I'd like nothing better than to take you back to Africa with me.'

Louise's eyes widened. 'Why?'

'I think you'd love it. I think you have the spirit for it. I think we'd make a wonderful team, that's why— No,' he cautioned, 'don't say a word. It's probably madness but at least it's honest.' He bent his head to kiss her briefly and hold her against him for a moment.

Then he set her free. 'Go to bed, Louise. I'll wake you in time for school, I promise.'

He didn't have to, as it happened.

She woke herself, saw it was a quarter to eight, relaxed and lay there as the whole incredible sequence of events filtered through her mind. Africa, she thought, with Richard Moore would be...incredible. As lovers and friends. Perhaps working on one of his documentaries, sleeping under canvas beneath the stars while lions roared around them, camp fires...

She closed her eyes. Until it came to a parting of the ways, as every indication so far pointed to. Am I that kind of person? she wondered. Able to take the moment, live it, then relinquish it? If you're disillusioned with love, is this not a better way to go? Or did I understand myself only too well when I vowed never to go into another relationship unless I was very sure it was with the right man, for the right reasons and would endure?

She was staring at the ceiling when a knock came on the door. She stiffened, then called, 'It's all right, I'm awake.'

'I've brought you breakfast,' Richard replied through the panels. 'Are you decent?'

She sat up abruptly, ran her fingers through her hair and looked around exasperatedly. 'I can come down if you give me a minute or two.'

'It'll get cold,' she heard him say, and the door opened. He shouldered his way in with a tray and brought it over to the bed. There was a glass of apple juice, a boiled egg and toast, a pot of coffee and a bunch of petunias in a small jug. 'It's not much,' he said. 'Just enough to get you going. We did have a midnight snack not that long ago.'

'Thank you,' Louise said with an effort. It was obvious Richard had been for an early morning swim. He still had his togs on beneath a T-shirt and they were damp. His hair was awry and he hadn't shaved.

'How do you feel this morning?' He pulled a chair up to the bed and removed the coffee and two cups from the tray to her bedside table.

Impossible, Louise thought, and amended the thought

to herself. *This* is impossible. 'An utter wreck,' she said tartly, 'but otherwise I'm fine.'

'You don't look an utter wreck.' He studied the luxurious disorder of her hair and the pretty blue camisole top of her pyjamas with its fine tucking and blue satin ribbon and bows. Then he looked around to say conversationally, 'Blue must be your favourite colour.'

'One of them,' she agreed. She'd used a delicate eggshell-blue as the predominant colour in her bedroom. The blue walls and carpet matched, the curtains and bedspread were ivory damask, the furniture was navy cane. But behind her bedhead there was a woven wall-hanging of flowers from coral-pink through to corn-gold.

'Coffee?' he said then. 'Your egg is soft, by the way.'

Louise took a deep breath and picked up her apple juice. 'You're—I feel as if I'm hitting my head against a brick wall,' she observed.

He raised an eyebrow. 'We're of the same mind, then.'

'I—remind you of a brick wall?'

'Mentally, yes. Physically, now that's another matter altogether,' he said gravely.

'Don't—'

'Start that? I wasn't going to,' he broke in peaceably. 'I'm here to suggest a truce. Let's start again, in other words.'

Louise put down her glass and picked up a spoon to decapitate her egg, which indeed proved to be soft but not too soft. She dug into it and ate most of it before replying. 'With what aim?' she said then.

'Friendship,' he said promptly.

'You know...this *is* amusing you!' Her green eyes were indignant and accusing.

'If you could have seen me trying to get to sleep from about three o'clock onwards, this morning, you might have known a different story, Louise,' he murmured dryly. 'But that's my problem, not yours.'

Their gazes clashed.

'And you...you think friendship is going to...to solve...that?' she said disjointedly.

'I don't know. I do know that I've committed myself to staying on and I do know why. I—'

'I couldn't just uproot myself and come to Africa with you.' She stopped abruptly and stared at him, not know-ing that the shadows in her eyes told their own tale.

'Yes. But if you'd let me finish,' he said rather gently. 'I don't want to turn this into a nightmare for either of us. A nightmare of misunderstanding and ill-feeling. I'd much rather we—become friends. So, if you can wipe the slate clear, I'll do the same. I'm moving out to a hotel today as—' his lips twisted '—proof of my good intentions.'

Louise's eyes widened. 'What will Neil think? Have you told him this?'

He looked at her quizzically. 'I don't think Neil is in any position to object, do you?'

Louise cursed herself inwardly for a foolish move, one that she didn't understand herself. She closed her eyes briefly and said, 'Can I ask you a favour? May I just get ready to go to school? I really don't think I can sort out *anything* in the short time I have available to me at the moment.'

'By all means,' he said with a perfectly straight face that didn't deceive her for a moment.

'You're laughing at me,' she said wearily. 'And don't

bother to deny it. You've been laughing at me ever since you came!'

'Have I?'

She paused and their gazes locked. It was she who looked away first with a tinge of pink entering her cheeks. The phone on her table rang. 'Neil,' she muttered, but was infinitely thankful for the interruption. And she added imperiously, 'Would you tell him I'm in the shower and in a rush to get to work? I'll deal with him this afternoon.' She pushed the tray and the bed-clothes aside and got up.

'Very well, Miss Brown.'

Louise opened her mouth, made a kittenish sound of extreme frustration and stalked away. When she came out of the shower, both Richard Moore and the remains of her breakfast were gone.

She didn't get the opportunity to deal with Neil for several days, as it turned out. Whether it was at Eve's instigation or Richard's, she didn't know, but the three of them spent most of their time on the Broadwater. The mention of jabiru plus the prospect of lovely sailing days had the other girl entranced.

As well as this, Louise discovered that she wasn't at all sure *how* to deal with Neil in light of what she and Richard had worked out. She found herself *not* dealing with him and actively avoiding him by manufacturing reasons to be out in the evening whenever she could. Richard had been true to his word and had moved out to the Sheraton, and Eve had moved in.

But she welcomed the breathing space, despite the fact that it was hard to go to work every day while the others planned such different days. Yet her state of mind was hardly peaceful, and during the few times they were all together she couldn't work out whether Richard's casual friendliness was harder to endure than having him remind her of their love making. And the one night Richard, Neil and Eve did spend on the boat was a dark and lonely time for her.

How could he? she wondered.

Neil and Eve had begged her to go, promising to deliver her back the next morning well in time for school. But the thought of spending a night on the *Georgia 2* had been too much for her, and she'd made some airy excuses.

In fact, she spent the night at home doing something she shouldn't have. It wasn't hard to find one of Richard's videos amongst Neil's collection and she watched it, to find that it was quite a revelation. Firstly, because she didn't normally watch conservation videos—one of the unfortunate side-effects of having the subject rammed down your throat, she'd thought ruefully—but, secondly, because it was so very well done.

This was no dreary sequence of animal shots, she discovered as she watched. This was the work of a consummate film-maker who not only created stunning visual effects but who also, with the use of people as well as the animals they lived or worked amongst, created humour, inspiration and pathos. A very complex man, was the thought she took to bed with her, and it wasn't a comforting one.

As she lay in the dark, unable to get him off her mind, knowing he was aboard the *Georgia 2*, for the first time since it had happened she allowed herself to remember that night.

Remembered being in the arms of a big man who used

his strength so lightly. Remembered the different tints of their skin in the cabin lamplight, the different contours of their bodies that had proved so fascinating and so completely satisfactory. So much so that for the first time in her life she'd offered herself proudly to a man and he'd made her feel so soft and silken, so slender and wand-like, so uniquely alive and sexy.

She remembered the wry smile they'd exchanged as they'd stripped their wet clothing off after that first, deep kiss—as if it was the most natural thing in the world. And how, in a dreamlike sequence, they'd come together, glorying in a physical release that was as powerful a symphony as the storm that had raged around them. Then the aftermath, lying cradled against that strong, streamlined body in a calm, warm haven.

I don't know what possessed me, she thought forlornly. I do know I'll never forget it...

Saturday came; but an inter-school swimming carnival was scheduled so instead of having a day off Louise finally left the pool with a headache. On her way home she called in to see Jane, who had left the hospital two days earlier.

Young Bradley was fast asleep in his crib looking most serene as they had a cup of coffee. Louise watched him for a moment, then turned to his mother. 'You're doing a great job, obviously,' she said warmly.

'Let's hope I can keep it up! So, tell me all your news. Has your uninvited guest departed?'

'No. What's more,' Louise said slowly, 'he turned out not to be a lame duck but Richard Moore, famed photojournalist and documentary maker.'

'Lou!' Jane sat up excitedly. 'I saw him interviewed once. He's gorgeous!'

'I'm afraid so.

Jane looked at her acutely. 'What does that mean?'

'Nothing,' Louise said hastily. 'But the real news is that Neil came dashing home on Monday with—hold on—a girlfriend in tow. One he's very serious about and they plan to get married.'

'How well does she know him?' Jane asked with a straight face, then dissolved into laughter. 'What's she like?'

Louise described Eve Parker. 'They're madly in love,' she finished, 'and despite the shock of it I can't help liking her.'

'So, is he staying? Richard Moore?'

'Yep. Well, he's moved to a hotel but they're all jab-iru-hunting for a fortnight.'

'Do you remember Roslyn White?' Jane asked.

Louise frowned. '*The* Roslyn White? The television presenter? Yes, she was gorgeous,' she said with a smile. 'Why?'

'They were an item, she and Richard Moore. Then all of a sudden she faded off the scene.' Jane wrinkled her brow. 'I always wondered what happened to her.'

'How interesting,' Louise said, quite nonchalantly, she felt, but the truth was, it had come as an unexpected shock to think of Richard and Roslyn White. Why? she asked herself as she saw that famous face in her mind's eye. Roslyn White had been a delight on television. Bright, bubbly, with a wicked sense of humour and a formidable intelligence, she had also possessed an en-chantingly heart-shaped face, heavy auburn hair, violet eyes and a petite, exquisite little body like a delicate ivory figurine. Because they'd have been perfect for each other?

'Uh—sorry,' she said, dragging herself back to Jane who had said something. 'What was that?'

'You wouldn't like to invite us round to meet him, would you, Lou? I'd adore to and I know Rob would as well.' Rob was her husband.

'Certainly,' Louise replied promptly and quite untruthfully, because she had absolutely no intention of giving her intuitive friend a chance to assess how things stood between herself and Richard Moore. 'I'll see what I can arrange. In the meantime, I guess I'd better be going. I'll come and see you in a few days.'

Neil and Eve were waiting for her when she got home and *this* time Neil, it appeared, was not to be avoided.

'Lou!' he said anxiously. 'What's going on? I never see you these days!'

Louise explained about the gala. 'I've shouted myself hoarse and given myself a headache,' she added ruefully.

'Well, just you sit down and put your feet up,' Eve said solicitously. 'I've made dinner. I thought if you didn't mind Richard in your kitchen you wouldn't mind me!'

Louise swallowed at the mention of Richard but made herself say warmly, 'Of course not. Talking of Richard, where is he?'

'He's having dinner at the hotel,' Neil murmured.

'I did invite him for dinner,' Eve said, 'but he wouldn't be budged. Never mind, it's probably a good thing until you two sort things out between you. Give her a drink, Neil,' she commanded. 'I'll call you when dinner's ready.' She waltzed out.

'You don't mind Eve being here, do you, Lou? It's an opportunity for *you* two to get to know each other,' Neil said earnestly. He opened the drinks cabinet and, without asking, poured Louise a gin and tonic. 'I can't tell you how sorry I am about breaking the news to you like that the other night,' he said soberly and handed her the glass.

Louise sank down onto a settee and took several sips. Then she put the glass on the coffee table and said quietly, 'Neil, all that matters to me is your happiness.' She paused to look at him searchingly and disturbed that shy but intent look in his eyes again—a look she'd never seen before, never thought to see for anything but zoology. She took a deep breath. 'If I've been—a bit confused, it's been because of the surprise of it. But I only have to look at you two together to know how you feel about each other and it's—wonderful to see.'

Neil relaxed visibly and came to sit opposite her, saying eagerly, 'When we're together, alone, it's as if there are only the two of us on the planet,' he said. 'Eve understands so much about my work and how I feel about things, we talk for hours! And she can be such fun—I never thought this could happen to me, Lou. I—never did,' he said simply. 'You know me.'

'I'm so very happy for you,' Louise could only repeat, with tears in her eyes because there was no doubt he was genuinely and deeply in love. Then she thought of Richard and added, 'Neil, one thing, though. You mustn't worry about me. One day my own true love will arrive on a white charger but until then I'll be fine!'

'There's something I have to tell you,' Neil said uncomfortably. 'I invited Richard up here for a reason. This is a little hard to explain but it kept occurring to me that you and he, well...' He stopped and looked at her helplessly.

'So we finally worked out,' Louise said a shade dryly. 'And that's what I meant about not worrying about me—'

'When did you work it out?' He looked surprised.

'Uh—a few nights ago. Richard didn't say anything to you?'

'No. Well, no.' Neil looked crestfallen. 'Just that he thought he'd be better off at the Mirage, but—' he hesitated '—you do like him, don't you? I mean, you have managed to sort things out, haven't you? Eve's not sure about that, but I—'

'Neil—'

'Dinner's ready!' Eve popped her head around the doorway.

Louise stood up gratefully, then she reached across and pressed her brother's hand. 'We'll be friends from now on, that's all. Gosh, something smells delicious!'

Delicious it smelt and tasted—paella with an especially bought bottle of sangria to go with it.

Conversation wasn't a problem as they ate. Eve was charming and amusing; she'd obviously gone to a lot of effort to impress her sister-in-law-to-be, but was also genuinely interested and obviously dying to know more about Louise.

So much so that Louise found herself responding with growing warmth and getting to like the other girl even more. But when the meal was finished and Louise offered to help with the dishes Eve said no, it was her night off; she and Neil would do them.

'What say we go for a walk afterwards, darling?' she asked Neil. 'I've got some clean sheets to put on the

Georgia 2. Like to come, Louise?' She smiled engagingly. 'Richard said he might be down there loading some supplies.'

But Louise was suddenly appalled to find that, much as she might like Eve Parker and happy as she was for Neil, it had just hit her how her life would be changing and how lonely it was likely to be from now on. Lonely because Neil and Eve would have each other whereas she would have—nothing. She swallowed and didn't see the way Neil's disturbed gaze rested on her face as she said with an effort, 'I think I'll pass. Have fun!'

In the event she did go for a walk, but to the beach, after changing into shorts and a blouse. So engrossed was she in deciding how she was going to cope that when someone loomed up in front of her she side-stepped him with a muttered, 'Excuse me,' not even realizing it was Richard until he put a hand on her arm.

Then she said wearily, 'Oh, no, not you! What are you doing here?'

'The same as you, I imagine,' he replied. 'Taking a walk after dinner.' He gestured towards the path that led to the Sheraton Mirage.

'But you're supposed to be loading supplies onto the boat! I wouldn't have come this way if I'd thought—' She stopped frustratedly.

'I had second thoughts about that. What's happened now?'

Louise stared at him tensely and willed herself not to say it, but it came out anyway. 'I can't believe how much my life has changed virtually overnight, that's all. It's—not my house any more, not my boat. I'm crying,' she said disbelievingly as she felt tears run down her cheeks and tasted them salty on her lips.

'Don't.' He took her in his arms.

She laid her cheek on his shoulder, then stiffened, but he said whimsically, 'Can I buy you a cup of coffee? It might just help.'

Louise lifted her head and suddenly found herself laughing.

'That's better. Come.' He took her hand.

CHAPTER FIVE

THE Sheraton Mirage Hotel on Seaworld Drive was within walking distance by road or by beach from MacRae Place. On its road frontage it was linked by an overhead walkway to Marina Mirage, a waterside complex of marvellous shops and restaurants with a distinctive roof created to look like white sails. And the marina, together with Mariners Cove, curved towards the Southport Yacht Club in the calm waters of the Broadwater, protected by a narrow finger of land called the Spit.

The beach side of the spit faced the might of the Pacific Ocean but the three-storey hotel nestled behind the dunes. As always, Louise thought as she followed Richard over the sand and through the gate, it was a delight to behold.

The vast complex of pools was lit from under water, there were braziers burning in the gardens and the main façade of restaurants, bars and lounges glowed behind huge plate-glass windows. She could see the fountain on the lower level of the foyer, see people dining by candlelight in beautifully elegant surroundings—and she stopped suddenly.

Richard turned to her enquiringly.

'I'm not very well dressed.' She looked down at herself.

He scanned her navy blouse, yellow shorts and yellow sand shoes. 'You look fine. You always do.'

'Thanks, but—'

He took her hand. 'Relax.'

They walked over the wooden walkways bisecting the pools, and then inside and up to the Breakers Bar. There was a pianist playing soft, dreamy music as they sat down in comfortable armchairs.

A waiter came immediately and Richard ordered two Irish coffees.

'So,' he said, 'the reality of Neil and Eve has suddenly hit?'

Louise interlaced her fingers. 'I'm being so stupid,' she said intensely. 'I'm so happy for him and she's trying so hard but I just…can't help…suddenly feeling like a displaced person.'

'It's only natural. Looking after Neil was a way of life.' He watched her searchingly for a moment. 'Have you, or rather how have you handled Neil's aspirations for us?'

Louise shook her head frustratedly. 'He came clean tonight—and you were right. I still can't believe it. Just to make life more complicated, Eve is in on the act and I don't think they've given up hope, despite me telling Neil that you and I were destined to be friends!'

'You have had a difficult evening,' he murmured.

Louise gazed at him. 'My best friend also thinks you're gorgeous, quote unquote.'

He raised an eyebrow. 'I've never met your best friend so—'

'She's seen you on television but, be that as it may, I'm suffering from a surfeit of praise for your manly properties— Why don't you tell me about Roslyn White?' she asked abruptly.

He frowned and said with a little edge to his voice, 'What exactly do you want to know?'

'Why wouldn't I want to know—' She broke off, seeing the trap too late.

He sat forward. 'Louise, are we going to be friends—or lovers?' he asked with his blue eyes penetrating, she felt, to the depths of her soul.

She looked away, then up, as the cheerful young waiter delivered their coffee and some delicious chocolates. When he withdrew, she said, 'I don't know. You see—' she took a breath and forced herself to look at him steadily '—I know *myself* rather well. What you said about Africa was—' she paused, swallowed, and then knew she could no longer hide the truth from this man '—the stuff dreams are made of. But I'm not that kind of person.'

He sat back but their gazes remained locked. 'What made you decide to tell me this now?'

She thought for a bit, then made an oddly helpless little gesture with her hands. 'Honesty. You accused me of trying to pretend it never happened. Because, you surmised, it had been such a revelation. You were right. At least, that was one aspect of it. The other *was* the deception you practised. I...I didn't know what to think. I was outraged. I'm still smarting, if you must know. But—' she looked away, then glanced back with a strangely proud little look in her eyes '—I'm basically honest once I—see things straight.'

'Thank you for that.'

'It doesn't help, though,' she said barely audible. 'It doesn't change *me*, or you.'

'It has to help towards understanding each other better,' he said after a time.

'Do you think so?' She leant forward to pick up her coffee glass.

'Of course.' He frowned briefly. 'What kind of a person are you so sure you're not?'

Louise drank some coffee and patted her lips with a napkin. 'Not the kind to act on a whim. To just throw up everything and follow you across the world would be a big step for most people. I know—' she gestured '—I know that what happened could be classed as a freak impulse, but to go on doing it...' She stopped and shrugged.

'Sometimes that's how people do fall in love,' he said.

'Do you seriously believe that?' Her eyes were wide.

He moved his shoulders and looked at her meditatively. 'I'd be inclined not to, but—' he paused '—you can't deny we were wonderfully matched in bed.'

'Are you trying to tell me it had never happened that way for you, either? Not even with Roslyn White? Or—there must have been other women?'

She saw his eyes change as soon as she mentioned the name again, saw a shutter come down that told its own tale, she thought. But she waited enquiringly.

'Strangely enough,' he said musingly, 'you're the only woman I've slept with, with not one word of conversation, Louise.'

'Could—?' She paused to cover the little jolt his words had caused her. 'You said you'd been in the Serengeti for a month. Could that have accounted for it from your point of view?'

He grimaced. 'You mean, was I so desperate for a woman?' His eyes laughed at her.

She tossed her head and said coolly, 'Would it be unknown?'

'Perhaps not,' he conceded. 'Had it been the case, however, it really would have been quite simple to acquire that kind of release.'

'Pay for it, you mean?' she said after a stunned little moment.

'Precisely, but don't hold it against me,' he said with irony. 'I'm not saying it's the kind of thing *I* do. I'm only pointing out that it would have been much easier and less complicated for someone in that position. What, incidentally, about your position?'

She shrugged offhandedly, but beneath his steady blue gaze a tinge of colour crept into her cheeks as his meaning became plain. 'Are you insinuating that I needed a man desperately?' she said hotly at last.

'Would it be unknown?' he answered softly, in a wicked parody of her earlier comment.

'For me,' she said through her teeth, 'yes.'

'Good. Then you admit that the unique chemistry between you, Louise Brown, and I, Richard Moore, was so powerful it overwhelmed us completely.'

She fumed silently for a moment, then said, 'You *should* take up law! But what you say doesn't change things.'

'Louise, if it had never happened I'd be forced to agree with you. But I think we're judging all sorts of things a little prematurely.'

'You'd rather wait until I did fall in love with you before you told me it couldn't work?' she suggested. 'Because you can't forget Roslyn, for example?'

'It isn't a case of not being able to forget her,' he said evenly. 'That's all over and done with. It is a case of being unable, at this stage, to predict exactly what would happen to us. For example, if you really want to know whether I'm good husband material—' his blue gaze was suddenly sardonic '—have you a particular test in mind?'

She flushed and finished her coffee uncomfortably.

'Do you see yourself as particularly good wife material?' he asked after a minute and with a wry little quirk to his lips.

'I...' Louise opened her mouth and closed it.

'Of course I have to agree,' he drawled, 'that you're domesticated, experienced with children, very decorative. The—er—extent,' he said with insulting delicacy, 'to which you're looking for a man whom you could smother with good works might pose a bit of a problem. I can't help wondering if that's why you liked me *then*, but don't seem to want a bar of me now. Are you that compulsive, Louise?'

Louise stood up slowly and carefully. Because what she really wanted to do was leap up and throw her coffee glass into his face. She said coldly, 'I'm going! Don't—'

'You can't,' he murmured. 'It's pouring.'

'I...' She stopped and turned to stare out of the window, to find the view obscured by teeming rain. 'When...?' She turned back to him wide-eyed.

'A short while ago,' he said comfortably. 'One of those sudden summer storms we seem to specialize in. Sit down, Louise.'

Louise sank down slowly with her nostrils pinched. 'So that you can continue to insult me?' she said bitterly.

'Forgive me, but your reasoning is a little hard to follow. You know,' he said quietly, 'it also would make things much easier for you if you didn't expose yourself too much to the inevitable dislocation arising from Neil and Eve's—union.'

'You mean,' she whispered, 'by going away with you?'

'Yes.'

'I can't. There's school, I...'

'And if there wasn't?'

She stared at him, then lowered her lashes abruptly. 'That's not fair, Richard.'

'Tell me.'

Her heart started to beat heavily because there was something so quiet and oddly gentle in his tone, it reminded her vividly of the quietness between them after they'd made love. A time of warmth, when the wonder had still been upon them and she'd felt safe—safe enough to fall asleep in his arms.

She made to speak a couple of times. Then she said simply, 'It would be heaven. But I still wouldn't do it.'

He was silent.

She waited, not knowing what to expect. The clever, satirical edge of his tongue? Something casual and dismissive, perhaps? But she managed to keep her eyes steady, although her hands twisted together of their own accord.

He said quietly, 'Let me get you home. It's been a long day, I think.'

Surprise registered in the way she blinked several times, then she licked her lips. 'How?'

'A taxi. There are always a couple out front.'

'I didn't bring any money.'

'I've got some.'

'Thank you.' She glanced outside a bit dazedly but it was still pouring.

'What did you think I was going to say?'

'I...I don't know,' she stammered. 'Something clever and uncomplimentary, I guess.'

'I think we may mean more to each other than you realize, Louise. Let's go and find that taxi.' He stood up.

Louise stared at him wordlessly.

He returned her gaze unemotionally, then he said almost curtly, 'I'm not a block of wood, unfortunately.'

She closed her eyes and got up abruptly.

But as he helped her into a taxi—there was indeed a line of them waiting on the concourse—he said lightly, 'Why don't you go straight to bed?' He leant in and conferred briefly with the driver and handed over some money. 'Sleep well.' He closed her door and turned away.

Back inside the foyer, Richard picked up an umbrella from Reception and walked through the downpour to the South Wing, where his room was on the top floor facing the ocean. The wide bed had been turned down and there were more chocolates on the pillow. The message light on his bedside phone was blinking and he made three calls in response to it, before he walked across the room to push the louvres aside and open a window.

He could hear the surf pounding on the beach as the rain eased and then, with all the contrariness of a summer storm, it stopped completely and a watery moon swam out from behind the clouds. He could also hear, he realized, the sad cry of a curlew. It made him think of Louise, alone in her blue bedroom with the fabric of her life so suddenly ripped apart.

He frowned and examined the thought that she was an enigma, this girl. So passionate, that once, and yet sometimes so unaware. So obviously content with what was an uncustomary existence for a twenty-five-year-old who was unusually beautiful. Surely one unhappy love affair hadn't achieved all that? he pondered.

He turned back from the windows, poured himself a drink from the mini-bar and took it over to the settee to think, dryly, that, like the walrus and the carpenter, the time had come to talk of many things—to himself, that was. Such was the unforgettable experience of the night on the boat—and now this. A girl who had admitted what she had tonight, but was still determined they could go no further. Because she can't forgive me for making a fool of her? he mused. Is all that wonderful passion inextricably linked in her mind with being deceived? I must have been mad but *I* can't forget it—and there was no thought of deceiving her as it happened. Or has she really convinced herself I'm the ultimate loner? On account of Ros?

He stared into space for a long time, sipped his drink and laid his head back to think, Am I? Surely I could just walk away from her if I was a loner... Or is there something else about her that touches me?

He smiled slightly. You were a revelation in bed, Louise Brown. It was as if that practical, ultra-capable, so determinedly benevolent side of you didn't exist. You were like a flame, ardent, proud, unashamedly excited, then quiet and sweet—everything you could want in a lover.

Is it, he wondered, that quality of wanting to help everyone that is so endearing? And is that the very reason you're so wary now? In case I am a lost cause?

He was staring into space again when the phone rang. It was Neil, agitated and disturbed because there was no sign of Louise. Would Richard have any idea where she might be? Her car was still in the garage, it was getting on for eleven o'clock and he was worried!

Richard frowned and glanced at his watch. Then he explained how they'd met on the beach. 'But I put her in a taxi nearly an hour ago. It should only have taken five minutes to get home. Look, I'll come round immediately.'

'Bad night,' the taxi-driver said. It was raining again. 'Mate of mine had a minor collision on this very stretch of road. Pouring cats and dogs, it was. You couldn't see your hand in front of you.'

'Did he have a passenger?' Richard turned to look at him sharply.

'Matter of fact, he did. The lady broke her wrist, they think. Had to cart her off to hospital.'

Richard swore aloud. 'Look, I think I know her. Take me to the hospital.'

'How…?' Louise, sitting in Casualty, looked up at the tall figure standing before her. 'How on earth did you…know?'

He took in her pale face, her swollen wrist resting on a cushion, and closed his eyes briefly. 'Neil rang me,' he said, and explained everything. He squatted down in front of her. 'I never should have sent you off like that. Is it very painful?'

'They've given me something for it. I was going to ring Neil, just in case he was worried, but I haven't had the chance.' She swallowed.

'I'll ring Neil now. No other damage?'

'No. Just a few bruises. It wasn't much of an accident—silly really. I put out my hand and—' she shrugged '—that's how it happened! But it's my right hand.'

'Never mind.' He stood up and dropped a light kiss on her hair. 'I'll be back.'

Two hours later they were in another taxi, headed home this time. The X-ray had shown one small bone broken in Louise's wrist and she had a plaster cast half-way up her arm and a sling. She'd been told to stay off work for a fortnight.

'It couldn't have come at a worse time,' she said anxiously as they drove home from the Southport Hospital. 'Exams coming up, the school concert—how could I have been so stupid?'

'It wasn't stupidity, just one of those things. It could have been much worse,' Richard said. 'In fact it was probably my fault.'

She glinted a pale smile at him. 'That's ridiculous. Anyone would think you'd sent me off to a war zone.' She put out her hand unthinkingly as the taxi turned a corner and gritted her teeth at the sudden pain.

Richard drew her back and put his arm about her shoulder. 'Keep still,' he said quietly.

She stayed rigid for a moment, then relaxed with a sigh and rested her cheek on his shoulder. 'There's something I ought to have told you tonight,' she said slowly. 'It was on my mind while I was waiting around for an ambulance and all the rest of it. I don't know why but, well, it was.'

'To do with us?'

'More in explanation, I guess. You said something about me being very experienced with children—'

'I'm sorry.'

'No, the thing is, you were right. But I deal with a lot

of children from broken homes because there *are* a lot of broken homes these days. I see the damage it does. I see a lot of girls who didn't have a constant father figure in their lives and the harm it does to them. I see exhausted, squabbling, separated parents who can't give their wayward children the one thing they need: security. I see kids who blame themselves...

'That's another reason why I'm so wary of landing in the same position. Although it doesn't apply to us, it tends to colour my thinking on the whole subject, I guess.'

He was silent.

She turned to look up at him eventually. 'I just thought...you deserved a fuller explanation.'

His eyes were curiously bleak as they stared at each other, then he kissed her lightly on the lips. 'Thank you.'

'Does it help?'

'One day it will— We're here.'

'Look, don't worry about coming in. You can take this taxi back.'

He paused to look at her narrowly. 'Why?'

She held his gaze steadily. 'I'm tired and emotional. I'm going to take the sleeping-pill they gave me as soon as I can get to bed.'

'I wouldn't stop you.'

'I know but there would have to be chat, you see, if you came in.'

But the decision was taken from her. Neil emerged through the gate with Eve hard on his heels, both very concerned.

'Too late,' Richard murmured with a wry little smile. 'But leave it to me.'

Twenty minutes later Louise was in bed, with only

her brother in the room. Getting undressed had been an awkward business even with Eve's help and that, combined with the pill she'd taken, on top of everything else, had exhausted her.

Neil put a pillow beneath her wrist. 'Sure you'll sleep now?'

'Yes. Don't worry about me, Neil,' she answered drowsily and smiled at him. 'I'll be fine.'

'But I do worry. Lou.' He sat down on the edge of the bed with concern—and guilt? she wondered sleepily—written in his eyes. 'I just want you to know that I won't be leaving you for a while yet.'

She frowned in bewilderment. 'What do you mean?'

'That you're my first priority, that's all,' he said intensely. 'You've been so wonderful about making a home for us and putting up with all my comings and goings, not to mention the trial I am most of the time. I couldn't bring myself to abandon you. And I know Eve will agree to us—postponing things for a time, because she's a very warm person and I'm sure she'll understand. So you just...relax.' He held her good hand tightly.

Am I dreaming this? Louise asked herself. 'Neil...' But her mind was already drugged and she found it impossible to think straight.

'I hate to see you looking so lost and alone, as you did earlier tonight when you were thinking about Richard,' Neil went on. 'And it's my fault because I tried to bring you two together. It's obviously not going to work. I'm not sure why. I didn't stop to think that he mightn't, well, want to embark on anything serious. I'm terribly sorry but *I'll* be here for you.'

He bent to kiss her lightly on her hair. 'If you need anything, give me a yell. Goodnight,' he said as she struggled to keep her eyelids open. He got up quietly and left her, waving once from the door.

I don't believe this—oh, no! What have I done now? But the powerful pill claimed her and she slept.

'You wanted to see me?'

Louise gazed at Richard, standing on the doorstep and there at her request. 'Yes, come in. Sorry, but...' She trailed off awkwardly.

It was ten o'clock the next morning. She'd slept until nine and awoken to see Eve peeping around the door. The other girl had then brought her breakfast and warmly offered to help her shower and dress. She'd also imparted the news that Neil had forgotten a special open-to-the-public lecture on conservation he was supposed to deliver at Bond University—forgotten it until the last moment, that was, so there'd been an unearthly rush to get him to it on time. That was where he was now.

Does she know? Louise found herself wondering a little frenziedly as the recollection of Neil's last words to her flooded her mind. But Eve made no mention and gave no indication that she had any idea she was about to be put on hold.

Then, when Louise was dressed, Eve had asked, if Louise was *sure* she could cope on her own for a bit, whether she'd mind if Eve grabbed a taxi and hastened down to Bond where she might just catch some of Neil's lecture. She so much enjoyed seeing him lecturing and there was to be a reception afterwards.

'Of course I don't mind. Look, you dash along; I'll be quite OK.'

'You're a pet,' Eve had enthused, and had kissed her.

It was in the sudden quiet of the house that Louise,

acting in pure desperation, had called Richard and asked him to come round.

'I—yes, I did want to see you,' she said again now, leading the way into the lounge. He had on another new shirt, she noticed, blue and green checks this time with a new pair of jeans. 'You're not going to believe what's happened.'

Richard raised an eyebrow. 'More drama? Sit down, Louise. And tell me how you feel before we launch into anything else.'

She swallowed and sat, supporting her wrist carefully. She was wearing a loose, sleeveless dress, green with little white flowers on it, flat green sandals and no make-up. 'I'm fine.'

'You don't look it.' He sat down opposite. 'Does it ache?'

'A bit, but—'

'Why don't you take a pain-killer?'

'I haven't had time! I'm just aghast—'

'Hang on.' He got up and left the lounge, to return shortly with a glass of juice and a white tablet. 'Take it,' he advised, 'and try to relax.'

Louise stared up the considerable length of him, then sighed heavily. 'Everyone keeps telling me that.'

'So they should.' He waited until she'd swallowed the pill, then sat down again. 'OK. What's happened now?'

She felt a bit of colour stain her cheeks and wondered if she'd done the right thing. Yet it had almost been a natural instinct to call on Richard, she realized, with a little jolt.

'Louise?'

She bit her lip. 'Neil is going to put off marrying Eve because he feels he can't leave me.'

There was utter silence for half a minute, then his lips twisted and he started to laugh softly. 'Bloody hell—When did this arise?'

'Last night,' Louise explained agitatedly.

'Does Eve know about it?'

'I'm sure she can't!' She explained about the lecture Neil had forgotten and the mad rush of the morning, as well as how serene Eve had appeared. 'But I'm sure she'd be hurt and find it hard to understand—I'm *twenty-five*, not some kid.'

'Are you sure Neil—?'

'Once Neil gets an idea into his head, it takes little short of an earthquake to dislodge it!'

Richard was still looking amused, to Louise's irritation. She added fervently, 'Look, I know him so well!'

Richard paused and frowned. 'How did it come up?'

Louise flinched inwardly. 'He said—he said I looked so lost and alone.'

'What did you say to that?'

'Nothing. I was half asleep. I'd taken that sleeping-pill and my brain felt like cotton wool,' she said bitterly.

'Well, did you feel lost and alone?'

Louise gritted her teeth. 'He thinks I'm lost and alone because of *you*.'

'Ah.'

'And he feels guilty because he brought you here!'

'I see.'

'That's no help!' she cried impatiently.

'Give me a minute,' he murmured. 'Unless—' he raised an eyebrow at her '—you have a plan of action already formulated?'

'How could I?'

'I thought for a moment you were going to suggest

that we run away to Africa.' There was a mocking little light in his blue eyes.

Louise made a strangled sound. 'I don't know why I thought you might be able to help!'

'Or did you think we could *pretend* to be serious about each other long enough for them to get married, thereby solving the problem that way?'

She looked around exasperatedly and her gaze fell on the flowers he'd bought her, still standing on the piano. 'I should change the water... Of course not! How could we?' She looked back at him with some irony.

'Perish the thought,' he said dryly. 'Uh, don't say it,' he advised as she opened her mouth.

'You can't know what I was going to say,' she objected.

'I can imagine. But there is something you may have overlooked—unless you feel Neil has a completely mistaken understanding of the matter?' He eyed her narrowly.

'What do you mean?'

'He got it wrong about you feeling lost and alone on my account?'

She coloured and could only say uncomfortably, 'So?'

'You don't think that indicates quite a degree of seriousness between us?'

The silence lasted a while as she tried to frame a reply. 'I...I...' she said at last. 'I told you why it couldn't work.'

'But we're not talking about starting a family, are we?'

'No, but that wasn't the only stumbling-block,' she returned tautly.

He smiled unamusedly. 'All right, you tell me what

we should do. You must have some ideas, otherwise why bother with me?'

'If we could…be friends,' she said haltingly. 'I mean *really*. So that Neil doesn't think I'm—'

'My dear—' he looked at her with a wealth of cynicism in his eyes '—I realize you're somewhat naïve but surely you can't be *that* naïve.'

'Am I?' She blinked rapidly. 'I didn't think I was.'

'Then perhaps I should spell it out for you. Having once run my hands over your beautiful body, having once touched your breasts and felt you arch your body beneath me, felt you quiver with sheer pleasure and welcome me with undisguised delight—all that makes mere friendship a little hard to contemplate. It always did, to be honest, but to have you tell me the things you did last night makes it—even harder. For me, although obviously not for you.'

Another silence fell as their gazes locked.

'You're wrong,' she said very quietly, and stood up to go over to the piano. She touched a rose, then turned back to him, standing straight and proud. 'I just can't afford to allow myself to—dwell on it. I'm sorry,' she added. 'I've been wrong to bother you with this—'

'I didn't say that.' He got up abruptly and came to stand before her. 'But you haven't shown it, Louise.'

She gestured a little helplessly. 'I've had an extremely turbulent few days one way and another.'

'Do you know what would happen if I kissed you now?'

'Yes,' she whispered.

'Tell me.'

She looked away.

'Perhaps I could tell you.'

'No... I...I'd love it, Richard,' she said barely audibly, 'but then I'd be in more trouble than I am now. Because I don't think I could stop myself from falling in love with you, and I don't think that would be at all wise. You think I'm naïve?' she asked huskily. 'Perhaps, but I know enough to know if that were to happen I'd be devastated when you left.'

Their eyes locked. He said slowly, 'You seem to be so very sure I would.'

'Shouldn't I be? Only moments ago we were talking about *not* starting a family. I know,' she said as he made a gesture of savage impatience, and she smiled faintly. 'I'm not damning you on the strength of that. I can't help but be aware, though, that, for whatever reason, getting deeply involved with another woman is not on your agenda. Am I wrong?'

'Louise.' He reached out and took her good hand, then sighed. 'No. It wasn't on my agenda.'

CHAPTER SIX

THE phone rang.

Louise swallowed and went to answer it. It was Neil, on his mobile. He'd just finished his lecture and was checking in, he said. How was she? Would she consider getting a taxi down to the university for the reception? He didn't like to think of her home alone...

'Neil, I'm fine,' Louise said, finally cutting across his rhetoric. 'No, really I am—don't you dare come straight home. Honestly, there's no need...'

She put the phone down at last and rubbed her face with her good hand.

Richard watched her and thought that, perhaps because of her wrist, she looked supremely vulnerable. And it was suddenly easier to understand Neil's concern. There was this accident, coming on top of another unhappy love affair for a beloved sister who was usually so capable but who had a heart of gold, and whom he worried about anyway... So, what to do?

He stirred. 'May I make a suggestion? How about a cup of tea? Why don't you sit in the garden? I'll bring it out to you.'

'You're a pal. I will go and sit in the garden. I feel as if I'm living in a lunatic asylum!'

He brought tea and biscuits out on a tray.

'Lovely, thank you,' Louise said as she sipped her tea. The canvas shade above the garden seat was warding off the heat of the sun but she could smell the grass and the camellias, and the sky above the sandy-pink wall was very blue. 'How is the jabiru search going?'

'We've postponed it for a few days. Neil suggested it last night after you'd gone to bed.'

'Oh, no.' She looked at him helplessly. 'I'm sorry. You'll be getting so bored.'

'To tell you the truth—' He paused and looked wry. 'I'd be happy to postpone it indefinitely. Being cooped up on a boat with a pair of *love* birds is not all that enjoyable.'

Louise's eyes widened, then her lips twitched. 'Go on,' she said gravely.

'Well, craven as it may appear, and only because I'm quite sure Neil and Eve would be just as happy on their own, I was about to invent an urgent call home. Jabiru were, after all, a bit of a subterfuge, anyway.'

Louise chuckled. 'Craven? I think you're perfectly entitled to go home with a clear conscience. This has been a—an absolute muddle from day one!'

'A disaster—you were going to say?'

'Y-yes.'

'Not entirely. What will you do if I go?'

'I have no idea,' she said after a long pause. 'Take it as it comes, I guess. Somehow or other I'll convince them they don't have to postpone getting married.'

'There is an alternative.'

His words hung on the air.

She swallowed and forced herself to look at him.

'I know I was rather scathing about your suggestion that we be friends, but it was something I suggested myself only a few days ago.' He smiled faintly. 'You're right about feeling as if one has strayed into a lunatic asylum. But for the next few days I'd be happy to try to dispel Neil's fears for you.'

So taken aback was Louise, she could only stare at him dazedly.

Until he said, 'You've had second thoughts?'

'No. No.' She had difficulty with her voice. 'I haven't had a chance to think one way or the other.'

'Then that's it. Will you have lunch with me?'

'Here? I—'

'No, if you'd allow me to drive your car and if you're feeling up to it, how about Mount Tamborine?'

'It's lovely up there,' Louise said involuntarily. 'Much cooler.'

'So I'm led to believe—I was reading some brochures. Do you know any good restaurants up there?'

'Songbirds.'

He raised an eyebrow.

'It's called Songbirds in the Forest. It's an indoor-outdoor restaurant and there are all these beautiful birds in the garden.'

'Then let's just go,' he suggested with a smile in his eyes. 'And let's leave all the trauma and sheer lunacy behind us.'

They did.

'I feel so much better,' she said as she ate a delicious lunch that Richard had cut up for her and they watched the lorikeets, rosellas and parrots in all their gorgeous plumage swooping and wheeling like rainbows on the wing. The air of Mount Tamborine was drier and cooler than on the Coast and because of this gardens flourished, there were waterfalls and deeply wooded, delightfully cool dells and pools. Tamborine Village was also a thriv-

ing artistic community with some lovely galleries that
sold pottery, paintings and bric-à-brac.

After lunch they wandered through the forest, then
drove to inspect some of the galleries.

'There's another lovely spot up this way,' Louise said
idly as they walked back to the car. 'Have you ever
heard of Binna Burra?'

'Yes. It was also amongst my brochures. A sort of
wilderness lodge, I gather?'

'It's part of the Lamington National Park. There are
lovely walking trails. Well, some of them are quite tax-
ing. It's very steep country, absolutely wild, yet the
lodge is really comfortable and the food is divine. Even
if you don't want to walk, just the views are marvellous.
A very good place for getting back to nature and re-
charging the batteries.' She stopped suddenly.

He looked down at her. 'Are you thinking what I think
you're thinking?'

I hope not, Louise said to herself. 'I...was thinking
that I might spend a few days at Binna Burra when
you've gone.'

But a tinge of colour came to her cheeks beneath his
steady, narrowed gaze and she knew that she'd given
herself away...

He put the key into the car door but didn't open it.
'We could do it, you know,' he said quietly. 'Just as
friends. Two nights.'

'I...don't think that would be very fair.'

'To whom?'

'Well—' her shoulders slumped '—both of us.'

'Oh, I think we could be adult and mature enough to
cope with two nights, Louise,' he said dryly.

Her head came up, for she'd been studying the

ground, and there was a startled, incredulous look in her green eyes.

'Besides which, I'm unlikely to take advantage of someone with a broken wrist,' he added. 'Would you like me to cross my heart and hope to die were I to lay a finger on you?'

A glint of anger replaced the startled look in her eyes. '*You* were the one who told me how difficult it was...it was...'

'So I did.' He smiled without amusement. 'I'm also the one trying to help you out of an awkward predicament. Let's agree to disagree about everything else— and I do agree that my immediate response to your suggestion was somewhat cynical—but surely this is an easier way to change Neil's mind? Rather than being in his constant company? You have my word, by the way,' he finished abruptly.

'I don't think Neil—I mean, I don't see how it *would* change Neil's mind.'

'Are you saying you'd be even more lost and alone afterwards, Louise?' he asked with irony.

She gasped and was conscious of feeling fighting mad suddenly. 'You should hope,' she retorted bitterly.

'Don't say yes, Louise,' he murmured wryly, then added briskly, 'Good. We'll do it now, then.'

'Do it now! Are you mad? We have no clothes, not even a toothbrush between us,' she objected angrily.

He looked around. 'There's a chemist and I'm sure we can find somewhere to buy a change of underclothes, a pair of shorts and a T-shirt. What else do we need for two nights? For someone who once told me she was a wilderness girl, are you now saying you need cosmetics, hair-rollers, perfumes, nail polish—?'

'I need a brush,' Louise said through her teeth.

'Then buy a brush.'

'I didn't bring any money!'

'History repeats itself—never mind, I did. So, are we going to do this or would you like me to assist you to scuttle back to your brother?' His blue eyes mocked her.

She said something unprintable but he only grinned at her and murmured, 'Now, now, Louise. Mind you, it's good to see a bit of spirit come back to you.'

'They may be booked out!'

He shrugged. 'There's a phone booth over there; let's find out.'

Binna Burra was not booked out and Louise stood, raging inwardly, as Richard booked two rooms. He rang Neil and passed on the news and at her urgent motions handed the phone to her. She took a deep breath, and managed to sound calm and composed enough to wring a promise from her brother that he would not do anything about postponing his wedding until she got back.

Finally, Richard handed some money to her and advised her to buy whatever she thought she might need, whilst he would do the same for himself.

He also said gravely, 'Perhaps we need to lighten up a bit, Miss Brown.'

Louise glared at the hundred dollars lying in her good hand, then replied with utter, false sweetness, 'All right, you asked for it, Mr Moore!' And she turned away to walk into the chemist.

She purchased two toothbrushes, toothpaste, a brush, a tube of moisturizer, a new sling and a packet of pain-killers because her wrist was aching. Heaven alone knows why, she reflected irritably, but the wilderness jibe got to me. So I will show him that I can exist for two nights on the basics.

Accordingly, she found a cheap pair of shorts and a T-shirt, a couple of pairs of panties and, because she knew that Binna Burra could be chilly at night, she purchased a light, cotton-knit pullover with long sleeves that had 'Mount Tamborine' colourfully printed across the front. She took her purchases back to the car, to find that she was there ahead of him but only just.

'No hat?' he said, strolling up beside her and glancing at the packages at her feet. 'Good. I found this one for you.' He'd been carrying it behind his back. 'Even a wilderness girl deserves a hat.'

Louise gasped again, this time with unwitting delight, because the hat he handed her was gorgeous. Not only that, wide-brimmed and made of raffia, the crown was swatched with a scarf tied at the back into a lush bow that was fashioned from the same green and white material as her dress. 'What a coincidence! Where did you find it?'

He pointed to a shop, then took the hat from her and put it carefully on her head. 'Good enough to go anywhere.' He touched a finger to her cheek. 'Shall we embark?'

So they drove high amongst the mountains of South-East Queensland to where the Binna Burra Mountain Lodge was perched in the Lamington National Park. The road was narrow and often tortuously winding, but as they got closer and left behind the more cultivated slopes of Mount Tamborine Louise couldn't help relaxing a little and found herself telling Richard some of the history of the rugged and beautiful area.

'Mount Warning, just over the border, is the remnant

of the centre of a huge shield volcano that threw up this jumble of peaks and ravines, apparently.'

'Captain Cook's mountain?'

'The same. Apparently a cyclonic kind of storm in 1770 threatened to blow him onto the rocks of Point Danger in line with Mount Warning and because it's so prominent and sheer and sharp he noted it as a reference to Point Danger. Then there's the legend of Bernard O'Reilly who found the plane that had crashed in the Macpherson Range in a similar kind of storm—he knew the area so well, which is incredible when you see what a wilderness of peaks and valleys it is.'

'Rain forest too,' Richard said, looking around at the huge trees beside the road.

'Yes, it's the most significant area of rain forest in this part of the state. I believe there are Antarctic beech forests in the really high country where it's often misty and cloudy, and then there's heath country and wild flowers and birds galore! You'll be sorry you didn't bring your camera. Lamington's famous for its birds— no jabiru that I know of, but bower-birds, lyre-birds, bell-birds. What a pity!'

'To be honest, again,' he said, 'I spend so much time behind the lens of a camera, I'm looking forward to absorbing all this without squinting through one eye. I think we're here.'

'Oh, I'm pleased!'

He glinted her an amused look. 'That we're here?'

'No—well, yes. But I'm pleased to think of you also being able to recharge the batteries.'

'Thanks,' he said after a moment as he nosed the car into a parking space beneath huge gumtrees. 'Shall I go and book us in? We might look a bit suspect bearing only a couple of shopping bags.'

Louise smiled suddenly. 'If you wouldn't mind. I'll wait here for you.'

It was quite a walk to their cabins but worth every minute of it. All the accommodation was in stone, timber and shingle cabins that blended unobtrusively into the hillside. The acacia cabins also had private amenities and their two adjoining cabins were the last you could come to, so they were not only the most secluded but their view over the Numinbah Valley was spectacular.

'Oh.' Louise let out a slow breath as she gazed out of the glass French doors.

'Now that is quite something,' Richard said softly from behind her. The sun was sinking as the afternoon waned and the clear air had a special radiance that gilded trees and peaks, and turned the depths of valleys to rose, amethyst and violet.

'I know this sounds almost mundane but we could make some coffee and sit outside to watch the sunset and listen to the birds,' he said quietly.

Louise turned to him. 'You have some brilliant ideas sometimes, Mr Moore.'

He looked at her gravely. 'I didn't think you altogether approved of this one, Miss Brown.'

Louise gestured and looked wry. 'I didn't, at first. It must be Binna Burra. I can't help—being happy to be here.'

He frowned. 'You're also looking tired and pale again—'

'I'm fine,' she said huskily, and felt her heartbeat trip, because there was genuine concern in his eyes. It occurred to her, with a suddenness that nearly took her breath away, that she could be quite wrong to turn away from this man, whatever his problems were. Because there was *something* between them that was so strong that, if he took her in his arms now, she would feel as if she was in heaven. Because she couldn't help longing to be there, secure, warm and filled with the kind of rapture only he had given her.

Why should I just accept defeat? she asked herself abruptly. He can't spend the rest of his life alone. Why am I so sure it can't be me who can change him? I've never thought of myself as a faint-hearted...

'Louise?'

She blinked and his face came back into focus, as well as the question in his eyes. 'Nothing. Uh—did you mention coffee? I could kill for a cup.'

He paused, as if to take issue with this evasion, but she turned back to the view and walked out to the terrace. It was all very well to make a decision, but to leap into it might not be. I've got two days, she thought. Two days to think this out very carefully, two days to find out if he does feel as strongly about me as I do about him.

When he brought their coffee out, she smiled her thanks and started to point out to him some of the peaks she recognized. When the sun had finally set and darkness was closing in, she asked him if he'd mind if she had a short rest before dinner, adding that he should prepare himself for a feast.

There was, she thought, just a hint of speculation in his eyes as he replied. But he left her without giving voice to it.

She lay down on the double bed and stared at the ceiling, suddenly gripped by uncertainty. Any fight to understand

Richard Moore would have to involve his past; she was sure of that from his unspoken reaction to any mention of Roslyn White... But what have I got to lose? she asked herself. *How* I lose him, if I do, is going to be immaterial, surely?

She slept for half an hour and would have slept right through dinner if he hadn't woken her by knocking on the door.

She sat up groggily and called to him to come in. But when he stood before her, showered and fresh in his jeans and checked shirt, she groaned softly and rubbed her face with her good hand.

A smile twisted his lips. 'May I make a suggestion?'

'Please do!'

'Have a shower while I make us a drink. We've got about fifteen minutes before the dinner gong goes.'

'Showering with one hand is extremely difficult and we don't have anything to drink,' she pointed out with some resentment.

'Yes, we do. I bought a bottle of Scotch in Tamborine. Scotch and water suit you?'

'Yes...'

'I can't offer to help you shower but I can help you in and out of your dress,' he added, quite seriously, although she knew he was amused.

'Thanks,' she muttered, and got off the bed. 'If you could just undo my zip.'

He complied and went away to make the drinks.

Louise commenced the difficult operation of changing, showering and dressing again with one hand. Even cleaning her teeth with her left hand was difficult. But she had to admit she felt better for it and she rubbed the moisturizer onto her face awkwardly and brushed her hair.

'This is a very basic me,' she said, padding out of the bathroom with a grimace. 'Can't imagine why I didn't bring a bag today—at least I'd have had a lipstick. Could you zip me up again and get the clean sling out of that packet?' She slipped her sandals on.

His fingers were cool on her back as he pulled the zip up. He then tied the sling. 'Comfortable?'

'Yes, thanks. Oh, damn!'

'What now?' He turned her to face him with a wryly raised eyebrow.

'It's getting a bit chilly. I bought a top but I'll have to take the sling off.' She looked down frustratedly.

'How about—? Is this it?' He picked up the top and smiled faintly at the colourful legend on it. 'How about putting it round your shoulders like this?' He draped it for her, tied the sleeves loosely in front over the sling and freed her hair. 'Once we get to eat you'll probably warm up.'

Louise didn't reply immediately for the simple reason that she was quivering inwardly at the feel of his fingers on her skin and aware, even from so light and impersonal a touch, of a trickle of arousal flowing through her body. Richard Moore, she thought, if you only knew what you do to me. She said, 'Did you say something about a drink?'

He turned to pick up a glass and handed it to her. 'May I say, Miss Brown, that your basic version is beautiful too? Cheers.' He picked up his own glass and wandered over to the glass doors to stare out over the darkness with one hand shoved in his pocket.

Louise sat down on the bed and stared at her drink.

'*Would* you—consider telling me about her?' Her lashes lifted abruptly and in some consternation, because she hadn't planned to utter those words, not now, anyway.

He turned back slowly and their gazes caught but he didn't pretend to misunderstand. 'What would you like to know, Louise?'

She raised her glass and took several sips. 'Only what you'd like me to know, if anything,' she said dryly. 'I don't propose to drag it out of you.'

'I...' He stopped as the dinner gong sounded.

'Saved by the bell,' she murmured, and drained her glass to stand up. 'This isn't the kind of place where dinner goes on for hours and hours. Shall we go?'

'And this mightn't be the right time to start an in-depth discussion either,' he pointed out.

'Oh, I agree. I'm not sure what made me bring it up right now,' she said, and shrugged. 'Whether there is ever going to be a right time is another matter. Are you hungry?' She picked up her room key and walked to the door.

He didn't move. 'Louise—'

'No, Richard.' Her green eyes were steady. 'Let's just go and eat.'

The dining room at Binna Burra had two levels, the lower level being much sought after for daytime eating because of the views. It also had a communal atmosphere—you sat where you could find seats, thereby getting to meet other guests, and the decor was rustic and charming. Because of all the outdoor activities most guests indulged in, appetites were keen and once the gong sounded the dining room filled up rapidly.

Richard found them seats at a table for six where four

other diners were already seated. As was the friendly
custom of Binna Burra, introductions were made and one
by one they ladled themselves pumpkin soup out of the
pottery tureen that stood steaming on the table. There
were also baskets of fresh rolls and home-made cob
breads on boards.

The others on their table were two couples, travelling
together, and it was their last night so they were in a
festive mood. They were keen bush walkers, it tran-
spired, and much interested in preserving wilderness
areas. It was the male partner of one couple who said
suddenly to Richard, 'I know you!'

'I'm sorry, but I don't—'

'No, we've never met, but you're Richard Moore,
aren't you? I mean, *the* Richard Moore.'

'Well...'

'That's it!' His wife smote her forehead. 'I thought I
knew your face. You make those marvellous documentaries. How exciting.' She leant forward eagerly.

Louise winced inwardly and wondered what she'd
landed Richard in...

Three hours later they managed to escape.

'I'm sorry,' she said helplessly as they walked towards the cabins.

He glanced down at her wryly. 'It wasn't your fault.'

'No, but I was the one who mentioned Binna Burra
in the first place. Some very keen naturalists come here.
It's the kind of place where you would be likely to be
recognized. It just didn't cross my mind.'

'Do you mean to say I've spent the past three hours
looking as if I was dying to be elsewhere?' he asked
with a grin.

'No. You were wonderful! But being introduced to a whole dining room full of people and asked to give a talk tomorrow night—well...' She gestured futilely.

'Look, don't worry about it. I can give these kind of talks in my sleep. Anyway, *I* care so it's good to see others doing the same.'

'Then you weren't dying to escape?' she asked. 'Underneath, I mean.'

'As a matter of fact, I was.' He stopped walking and took her good hand.

She looked at him with an uncertain query in her eyes.

'Because you're angry with me again, Louise,' he said quietly, and his blue eyes probed hers narrowly.

'If I was, that was three hours ago,' she said on a breath.

'The thing is, I'm not sure what's going through your mind. If—' he paused '—you were angry because I didn't appear to be forthcoming on the subject of Roslyn, I can't help wondering why.'

Louise bit her lip. 'This—again, this is not a good time to be delving into it,' she said at length. 'Could I ask for an extension?' She tried for a bit of humour, but the smile she attempted to pin on her lips was only a shadow of one.

'All right.' He studied her, then released her. 'Need a hand?'

'Just with my zip,' she said tiredly.

He unlocked her cabin for her and came in. 'I believe there are extra duvets and electric blankets if you need them.' He opened a cupboard and pulled down a duvet to lay over the bed.

Louise grimaced. 'I might. Didn't think to buy pyjamas.'

'Neither did I,' he said wryly as he dealt with her zip and, as an afterthought, released her bra. 'This must be a real hassle to get in and out of.'

'You're not wrong,' Louise murmured, and turned to face him, holding her dress up awkwardly as it started to slip off her shoulders. 'Thanks.'

'Would I get my face slapped if I suggested helping you into that T-shirt?' he gestured to the shirt and shorts she'd purchased. 'Unless you prefer sleeping in the altogether?'

'I loathe sleeping in the—' She broke off and bit her lip.

'It does seem rather pointless when you're on your own.' His lips twisted. 'All the same—' He stopped suddenly, stared into her tormented eyes, and something changed in his at the same time. She thought he sighed inwardly. 'I'll go. Goodnight.'

He left abruptly.

There was a mist swirling through the valley when Louise woke the next morning. A sun-bright mist that hurt the eyes and hid the view.

She didn't leave her room until she heard the breakfast gong, nor venture onto the terrace which was right next door to Richard's, but she did expect him to knock on her door. No knock came, however, and when she tried his door there was no response.

She shrugged and started up the path towards the dining room. Up above the valleys that surrounded them there were only a few curls of mist and sunlight shone on the gardens of Binna Burra. There was a lawn outside the dining complex with trees for shade, and tables and chairs. It was a lovely spot to relax and overlook the country, a place where butterflies danced and noisy little pitta-birds sang.

That was where she found Richard, standing almost at the edge of this peaceful plateau, staring into space.

'Good morning,' she said quietly. 'I wondered whether you'd decided to desert me.'

He swung round after the barest hesitation, but one that she couldn't miss. It made her eyes widen because she hadn't spoken in seriousness; it had just been something to say. Yet it seemed as if she'd touched a nerve...

'Morning,' he said lightly, though. 'Sleep well?'

'Not too badly. How about you?'

'Not too badly either. Shall we go in?'

'I've been thinking,' Louise said as they finished their breakfast and sat over coffee. 'Why don't you do one of the walks? It's a pity to be here and miss out. I'll be quite happy to find a book and listen to the daisies grow, so to speak.'

He sat back. 'How is the wrist?'

'Fine,' she lied. 'Just not up to hiking in this kind of country.'

'You could probably handle the Senses Trail.' He pulled a brochure from the pocket of his shorts.

'I'm sure I could, seeing it was built for blind or blindfolded people, but it only takes about half an hour. Wouldn't you like to do a real walk?'

'I,' he said with a grimace, 'have decided to go abseiling this afternoon. The conditions are good; they predict the mist will clear. So I'd be happy to escort you round the Senses Trail first.'

'How brave,' she commented. 'That's fine, then. I don't have to feel guilty about bringing you to Binna

Burra only to sit around. *Were* you planning to—?' She stopped abruptly.

He'd bought himself a blue T-shirt that matched his eyes and he wore it now with navy shorts. It struck her suddenly that he looked fit and strong, keen and alert. By contrast she felt drab and colourless, even in her new shorts and T-shirt that had taken quite some effort to get into.

'Was I planning what, Louise?'

She finished her coffee. 'To desert me? I thought it must have crossed your mind from the way you hesitated, earlier.'

His gaze was level but tinged with irony. 'Abandon you here, Louise? Did you honestly think I'd do that to you?'

'Go away from me in some form or another?' she said barely audible. 'Yes.'

'Have you changed your mind about us?' he asked ironically.

'What makes you think that?'

'We're attempting to "go away" from each other amicably, after all, are we not?' he said dryly.

Louise felt her skin prickle with irritation. 'Is it any wonder, Richard? It's like dealing with a brick wall; it always was and it still is. Look, you do whatever you want; I'm going to find myself a book.' She stood up and walked away angrily.

He didn't attempt to follow her.

She spent half an hour in the shop, then found herself a book from the library and took it back to her cabin, only to find a maid doing the room. So she got her hat and went out onto the terrace, where she pulled a chair into the sun and sat down to read.

But the words blurred, and to her humiliation she found herself indulging in a good, old-fashioned cry.

And that was how Richard found her, staring unseeingly at the view with silent tears streaming down her face.

CHAPTER SEVEN

HE SAID nothing for a long moment, then squatted down beside her and handed her his hanky.

'Thanks.' Louise wiped her eyes and sniffed. 'Sorry about this. I think I'm feeling sorry for myself in all directions this morning. I'll—get over it.'

'Come for that walk.'

She looked up at him wearily. 'It's not exactly what I feel like doing at the moment, Richard, so—'

'I thought we could sit down along the way and discuss Ros.'

Her drenched eyes widened.

'That is what you're in a state about, I gather?'

Louise bit her lip, then blew her nose vigorously. 'Put like that, I don't think I want to know after all.'

'Nevertheless, if we're ever going to understand each other—you're right, it needs to be said.'

'What—' she frowned up at him '—brought about this change of heart?'

'I thought *you* might have had a change of heart,' he said quietly.

Louise sniffed again and her shoulders slumped. 'Not the kind you're hoping for, I would imagine.'

He stood up abruptly. 'Let's go.'

They found a bench along the path of the Senses Trail. It had been built, this trail, to give blind people an easy, safe passage so that they could experience some of the magic of the bush, particularly the bird-song and the

144

scents of the forest. There was a Braille brochure keyed
to signs along the way and a guide rope. The trail was
not only used by blind people but by blindfolded walkers
eager to focus their other senses on the environment.

The trail was deserted as Richard and Louise sat in
dappled sunlight. Birds were singing and the dense green
foliage around them rustled as a breeze stirred it. Then
it was still and hot, and cicadas alternately shrilled and
fell silent as if there were a choirmaster directing their
symphony.

'Want to go first?' Richard asked.

Louise gestured irritably, then sighed. 'It suddenly occurred to me I was giving up on you without a fight,'
she said bleakly and directly.

His lips twisted.

'I don't know why I didn't realize that would amuse
you,' she said wearily.

'Only because it's so beautifully frank.'

'Yes, well, let me be franker. I still would not be
content to merely go for an affair. It's either all or nothing.' She gazed at him moodily and added with further
irritation, 'Now you've trapped and *goaded* me into
sounding ridiculous and as if I'm expecting a wedding
ring this very moment.'

'I hesitate to be argumentative but that's what it did
sound like,' he said meekly but with a devilish little glint
in his eye.

'Well, you're wrong. What I require is for you to at
least acknowledge that it's not out of the bounds of prob-
ability for us to end up—together.'

'That sounds much more sensible,' he agreed.

'Oh, but don't be taken in,' she warned. 'Because I
would know if you felt differently from how I felt. In

other words, I wouldn't be content to be your Australian mistress, or one of them, whilst you happily beetled backwards and forwards between MacRae Place and Africa.'

'I don't have any mistresses, Australian or otherwise.'

'How do you cope?' She raised an eyebrow at him.

'It's possible, you know,' he said gravely.

'Casual sex, you mean?' She eyed him and was rather pleased to detect a flicker of annoyance in his eyes.

'When—' he paused '—*if* it happens on a non-permanent basis, Louise, I try to avoid being at all casual about it.'

'So you've devised a way of sending them away—'

'I haven't devised anything,' he broke in with sudden savage impatience. 'There've been a few occasions when it's happened with mutual need, on a no-harm-done basis and with good humour.'

'I've made you angry.' She looked at him reflectively. 'I'm glad—no, I've been feeling the fool in all this for too long, Richard. I've also been the ''show and tell'' event for too long. It's your turn now but we can do it that way if you like— Is Roslyn White the reason you're a loner?'

She saw him grit his teeth, then he said evenly, 'It's probably a combination of things, Louise. The débâcle of my parents' marriage, a career that makes any kind of a relationship difficult, let alone marriage.' He stopped and shrugged.

'But every time I mention her name you—I can see you change,' Louise said quietly. 'There has to be a reason for it. I gather it wasn't a non-permanent, no-harm-done, with humour et cetera relationship?'

'How did you get to know about her in the first

place?' he parried, and frowned. 'You obviously didn't know me from a bar of soap.'

'My friend Jane—the one who's just had the baby—she keeps up with all the gossip. I went to see her again the day before yesterday. I hadn't told her your name the first time but as soon as I did—'

'She proved to be a mine of information?'

'Yes. And—' Louise paused and gestured '—once I knew, I couldn't help thinking how...well you two would go together. She was lovely.'

'She still is,' he said after an age. 'She is also my brother's wife now.'

Louise gasped. 'But why? I mean...' She trailed off awkwardly.

'Oh, I think she worked out that he was a much better bet than I was,' he drawled. 'Gareth is not one to hide his light under a bushel. He's a very prominent businessman, he has a home in Sydney, a flat in London and a beach house at Noosa. He enjoys foreign sports cars and he owns racehorses—all the things that mean zilch to me. Ros will have a very busy social life, be quite the little queen bee in fact. And will be able to continue her career at the same time, eventually.'

'But...but how come *this* is not common knowledge?' Louise stammered, and flinched as he cast her a look that spelt out just how trite a comment it was.

He said, 'Gareth had to divest himself of his first wife in order to acquire Ros, that's why.' He grimaced and looked fleetingly amused. 'My parents, so seldom united about anything, took a joint stand on this one, much to our collective amazement. They insisted that, on top of my involvement with Ros, Gareth getting a divorce—he and his first wife have three children and she was distraught—was a bit much to be flaunted too publicly. So Gareth and Ros retired overseas whilst all the murky details were got through.'

Louise swallowed. 'His first wife was distraught?'

Richard glanced at her unemotionally. 'And angry enough at first to want to shout out all the wrongs she's suffered to the world. If anyone was the loser in all this, it was Julia.'

'Does that mean to say that Roslyn White is...is...?' She looked at him, bemused.

'Very lovely, but about as cold and calculating as a snake? Yes. It's strange how looks can deceive, isn't it?' His expression was coldly quizzical.

Louise mulled over it all dazedly. 'Are you telling me she threw you over for your brother for a *lifestyle* and prised him apart from his wife in the process?'

'That about sums it up,' he said dryly. 'Not that Gareth was by any means innocent himself. Julia was probably the only one who didn't know that he had been having affairs for years. But where he may have been a little unlucky was that he didn't realize what a spur it was to Ros when *I* refused to change my lifestyle for her.'

'She—it was revenge?' Louise's eyes were wide and horrified.

'So she told me.'

'But your brother doesn't know this?'

'Hardly.' He looked at her ironically.

'So what will happen—a few years down the track?' Louise asked dazedly.

'Your guess is as good as mine. But I should imagine that unless a much bigger fish comes along there'll be ample compensation for being Mrs Gareth Moore instead of Mrs Richard Moore.'

'That's awful,' Louise breathed.

'If you're imagining I'm distraught and bereft, you're wrong,' he said coolly. 'I told you, it was over. Except that I shall always feel guilty towards Julia and the kids.'

Louise thought for a bit. 'Well, I'm sure you could never trust Ros again, but—' she turned to him helplessly '—*can* you stop wanting someone you can't have? I mean, in your own secret self, is it not sheer hell imagining her—with your brother?'

'I got over that,' he said wryly.

'Then why are you the way you are?' she demanded.

'I couldn't change myself for her, Louise. As it's turned out it's just as well, but—that's got to mean something.'

There was silence for a long time.

Then he added, 'To be fair it's no small thing to ask, to expect someone to want to spend their *life* doing what I do. I know it may seem romantic to the right kind of person in the short term. The long term is a different matter.'

Louise licked her lips. 'When the children come along, you mean? Yes—' she waved him to silence '—I can see that. Will you always want to be roaming the wilder parts of the world?'

'I imagine so. I think it's in my blood.'

'So you don't visualize ever marrying?'

'I'd be a fool to make cast-iron decisions in that regard.'

'I…' Louise closed her mouth as something prompted her not to utter what had come to mind. The thought that Richard Moore was using his lifestyle as an excuse.

But, if so, why? Because his disinclination to get deeply involved with another woman stemmed more from the trauma of Roslyn White than he was willing to admit? Got you, she thought to herself. Then she sighed inwardly at another thought: Where does it leave me?

'You were going to say...?'

'I don't know; I'm still a little stunned, I guess,' she confessed, not altogether accurately.

He smiled faintly. Then the smile faded. 'If I appeared unwilling to discuss this, perhaps you can understand why now?'

'Yes,' she said, but distractedly. Then she made an effort to concentrate. 'Your story is quite safe with me. I wouldn't tell another soul.'

'Of course—I didn't doubt that. But it doesn't make pleasant hearing.'

'It doesn't help me much, either,' she said. 'Us much.'

'Would it—' he paused and leant forward with his hands between his knees '—reassure you that you would be the only woman in my life?'

She watched him, the line of his shoulders under the blue T-shirt, the long muscles of his back, his profile. 'I may have to think about this.'

'You don't believe me?' He didn't turn his head.

'Yes, I do believe you, but I don't think that's enough for me.'

He sat back and looked at her at last with his blue eyes curiously sombre.

Louise drew an unsteady breath and continued, 'It's not that I want you to change yourself for me, but because you lack the faith to believe I could—cope. Or that *we* could cope. I have also...' she hesitated '...I may have misled you to a certain extent.'

'What about?'

'In letting you think I was disillusioned— Well, I was, that's true, but what happened reinforced another theory of mine, I'm afraid.' She swallowed and wondered how to proceed without sounding extremely foolish.

'Go on.'

She clenched her good hand into a fist and took the plunge. 'I'm a great believer that love conquers all, you see. When you find it, that is. I know you don't see it often but...' She stopped, then shrugged. 'I like to think of Shah Jahan and Mumtaz Mahal and all the other great love stories. I—that's what I would like to mean to a man.'

It caused her a shaft of pain to see that she had arrested him completely. She said, to cover it, with a wry little lift of an eyebrow, 'I guess I didn't come across as a romantic?'

'Not—entirely.'

'Not at all, you mean.' She grimaced. 'Too busy being a do-gooder, I guess.'

'Louise—'

But she stood up. 'Richard, thank you for telling me all you have. I don't know why but it makes me feel a lot better. I guess I was...well, feeling baffled. Then I thought I was being faint-hearted not to want to fight for the right to build something out of what we feel. Now I know that only you can live with yourself and all that's happened, as well as your hopes and dreams, just as I can only do the same.'

'What does that mean?' he queried.

'That I'll have the composure and tranquillity to go back to Neil and reassure him I've got over you,' she said quietly and steadily.

'Bloody hell.' He stood up at last with a mixture of disbelief and savage impatience warring for supremacy in his expression.

She took a step backwards and tripped. She would have fallen if he hadn't grabbed her.

'I'm f-fine,' she stammered as he continued to hold her. 'Why are you looking at me like that?'

'Because you defy description sometimes, Louise,' he grated. 'You have this ability to turn yourself off from me. Do you know how infrequently there's a Shah Jahan for every Mumtaz Mahal? I would have thought you had more sense, if nothing else.'

'No, I don't know that,' she shot back. 'Shah Jahan just did things on a grand scale! I do know, for example, that my father never remarried because he never got over my mother! It *happens*.'

He swore again. 'And this happens.'

'Don't—'

But he did. He positioned her wrist out of harm's way round his waist and started to kiss her.

'Richard—'

'Shut up,' he ordered roughly. 'And then you can tell me how it compares to having a Taj Mahal built for you.'

'You bastard,' she breathed. 'You *know* what I meant!'

'I know you're living in dream-land,' he retorted, and claimed her lips.

Louise struggled for a few moments but he resisted all her efforts. When they came up for air finally she was close to tears—tears of frustration because she'd ended up kissing him back with extreme, albeit angry passion.

They stared into each other's eyes, oblivious of anything around them, both caught in a net of desire. Desire whereby to breathe was to inhale the heady scent of each other's skin, where every point of contact between their bodies was a contrast between the strong, hard-angled planes of his and her softer curves. Desire which produced in Louise a rush of quivering arousal. A desire, at the same time, to fight this fight to the finish...

'If there was a bed or a bunk handy you know what would happen now, Louise, don't you?' His lips barely moved and his gaze dropped to the swell of her breasts beneath the T-shirt. He traced the outline of one swollen nipple and felt the response quiver through her body, saw the way her lips trembled and how the pulse at the base of her throat raced.

'We'd be in the position of not being able to help ourselves again,' he went on with unmistakable satire. 'I'd take your clothes off and you'd offer all that slim, satiny ivory and rose velvet body to me, all those secret, shadowed places to me just as you did before. Doesn't that mean anything?'

'All it means is that you want me in bed,' she answered huskily.

'As you want me.' His eyes mocked her. 'Don't you remember the things you did?'

'All too well. All it got me,' she said with sheer hostility in her eyes, 'is someone too cynical to appreciate me other than in mistress terms.'

'You were the one who tried to pretend it had never happened,' he taunted. 'I'm the one who has never, it so happens, mentioned mistress terms to you or any other terms because—'

'Because you're the one who doesn't realize just how

deep your aura of solitariness is!' she retaliated. 'No one in their right mind would get...would experience that with you and not know they were headed for disaster.'

'Excuse us,' a strange voice said, causing them both to start. They turned together to see two blindfolded people on the path behind them. 'We didn't want to disturb you, but...'

'I'm so sorry,' Richard said. 'Uh—the path is clear now.' He drew Louise aside.

'Lovely day!' one of the walkers enthused but with an overtone of embarrassment as they groped their way past.

'Beautiful,' Richard and Louise agreed, and watched them out of sight.

'At least they won't recognize us,' Louise said. 'I feel an absolute fool!'

He glanced down at her wryly. 'I wonder how long they waited?'

Louise cast her mind back over the things said and began to colour hotly.

He touched a hand to her cheek lightly. 'Never mind; as you said, they couldn't see us.'

'They could recognize our voices,' she said hollowly.

'Ah, but we can recognize them, so all we have to do is steer clear of them.'

'Don't forget you're giving that talk tonight!' she reminded him.

He swore softly, then started to laugh. 'I might have to acquire an accent.'

'I don't think this is funny at all!'

'I've noticed that—the times you seem to lack a sense of humour,' he said wryly.

Louise muttered something beneath her breath. 'That

could be because I'm always the one in the hot seat,' she said bitterly. 'I didn't describe your body in...in...' She stopped abruptly.

'In all its splendour? Talking of yours, I mean. It was all true, though, you know.'

'Let's not start that again,' she said with some agitation.

'What do you suggest?' He studied her amusedly.

'Going back,' she replied tartly.

'So you can think more about whether you want to fight me, sleep with me, do *both*, or run home to Neil?' he asked idly. 'Seems to me all that composure and tranquillity got lost somewhere along the line.' He raised an eyebrow at her.

Louise bit her lip and curbed an impulse to hit him. 'This is your male ego talking, you know,' she said, however, with an ironic little glint in her eyes.

'Oh, definitely,' he agreed.

'It's obviously not as adult and mature as you think!'

He looked down at her with a wicked glint in his eye. 'If you really want to do a Mumtaz Mahal you probably shouldn't ignore these opportunities, Louise.'

'I'll never confide in you again,' she said through her teeth.

'That's a pity,' he said. 'It opened a whole new insight into you.'

'One that you obviously find ridiculous,' she said moodily. They were walking now.

He took her hand and refused to release it as she tried to pull away. 'It's all right,' he said gravely. 'My male ego is under control again.'

She said nothing.

'No, it's not that I find it ridiculous—'

'You were pretty scathing about dream-land.'

He glanced down at her but as they walked she kept her eyes downcast. 'I don't suppose it happens that often.'

'Perhaps not,' she conceded. 'That doesn't mean to say it can't.'

'Do you think Neil and Eve have it?'

Louise frowned, then, unwittingly, a smile came to her lips. 'I think they do. He—' she shrugged '—told me that when they were alone it was as if they were the only two people on the planet. They can talk, you see. He said he can tell her about all his dreams and so on.'

'We've only really had one day when we've done that,' Richard commented.

'On the boat?' She raised her eyes to his briefly. 'Yes, well, we didn't exactly go into our dreams.'

'For which I'm never to be forgiven,' he said wryly.

'Perhaps that's what comes from putting the cart before the horse.' She paused. 'Ever since it happened it's been—' She broke off.

'All trauma,' he said a shade dryly.

'Would you like to be able to turn back the clock?' she asked abruptly.

'I'm beginning to wish I could... We're here.'

'What will we do now?' she said as they came to the end of the walk.

'Have a drink before lunch? That seems a fairly ordinary, civilized thing to do.'

An odd undertone caused Louise to study him narrowly. 'Are you suggesting we've been uncivilized?'

His lips twisted as he stood before her, tall and golden in the sunlight. 'We've visited some sordid depths and outer, legendary realms, we've been made to feel foolish and didn't quite manage to keep our hands off each other—I think a drink is definitely called for, if nothing else. Sit down.' He indicated a chair on the lawn. 'I'll bring you a glass of wine.'

'Richard.' She took a breath. 'No, nothing.'

'Say it.'

Their gazes clashed.

Louise gestured helplessly after a long moment. 'I'm all of a muddle again, that's all.'

He smiled faintly and fiddled with a strand of her hair, pushing it behind her ear eventually. Then he kissed her lightly on the brow. 'Stick to your dreams,' he said very quietly. 'I actually admire you very much for that, despite having intimated to the contrary.' He turned away to walk up to the dining room.

The rest of their stay at Binna Burra was curiously peaceful for the most part. Louise spent the afternoon reading and resting with her mind oddly blank while Richard abseiled, then they dined sumptuously again.

It was while Richard was giving his talk that she felt unsettled. As she watched and listened to him describing Serengeti, the Masai Mara and the great migration of game that took place annually; as he, with no videos or even maps and pictures, brought alive wild Africa in all its glory and with all its problems, she was absorbed, as was everyone. But at the same time she was conscious of a sense of loss and failure.

Because Richard Moore revealed more to her in this talk than at any time since they'd met. He revealed his dedication, his understanding of the problems of people who had to live alongside wild animals or be shunted off their traditional lands so that game could be preserved. Also his understanding of people reduced to a bare existence by drought and other factors, who poached for ivory, people from whom others made a fortune.

He was humorous, eloquent—he managed to paint with words the images he captured so successfully on film—and utterly compelling.

He held the guests of Binna Burra in the palm of his hand and Louise knew, from the rapt expressions around her, that they would take away with them not only some of his own concern but the memory of a man who combined wisdom, compassion, strength and a rare magnetism.

'That was—so good,' Louise said as they wended their way back to their cabins. It had taken half an hour to extricate themselves, although Louise had waited quietly on the sidelines as Richard's audience had crowded around him.

'Thank you.'

'You sound tired now.'

He grimaced. 'I don't abseil down cliffs every day.'

'But it's fun, isn't it?'

'You've done it?'

'Yes.' She smiled. 'Once I got over my fear that I was going to tip upside down and land on my head, I loved it.'

'I might have known,' he said wryly. 'I suppose you're also into ballooning, hang-gliding and parachuting?'

'No, not yet, but I'd love to try. I don't know about parachuting and hang-gliding, but ballooning, yes,' she said enthusiastically.

'You can do a balloon safari over Serengeti,' he said.
'They take off at dawn from the Masai Kopjes, just as
a papaya-pink sun is coming up and all the game is
stirring. It's a unique sensation. I think perhaps one of
the most unusual parts of it is sailing over these huge
bird's nests. The birds don't panic, they just look up at
you, faintly curious.'

'Richard—' They'd reached their cabins. 'Come in for
a moment,' she said.

He looked at her with a faint frown, then shrugged.

'Sit down,' she invited a few moments later as she
turned on the lamps. 'Would you like a cup of coffee?'

'Thanks—I'll do it.'

She sank down herself and watched him thoughtfully.

'What is it?' he asked with a rueful tinge as he placed
her coffee beside her and sat down himself. 'You look
very serious.'

'I just wondered—would you tell me—? I mean, it's
rather strange for an Australian to have such a strong
fascination for Africa. I'm just wondering whether something in your upbringing fostered it or— How did it
happen?'

He frowned. 'There's an old saying about Africa; once
you get it in your blood you can't get it out.'

'I know that. I've read Karen Blixen, but hers was a
rather different reason for going there in the first place,
wasn't it?'

'Following the man she was to marry? Yes.' He
paused. 'I think it was something to do with proving
myself to my father that started it all,' he said. 'Art or
any artistic bent was something he was always irritated
by. I was spurred along by my mother; she's an artist—'
he gestured '—she paints. She's very successful, al-

though I have to admit she can be madly eccentric at times.'

Louise's eyes widened as this sank in. 'He didn't appreciate you following in her footsteps? But—'

'This is different? You were going to say?' he supplied.

'Isn't it?'

'Of course, in lots of respects. It combines science and technology as well, but without a creative eye you can employ all that and achieve nothing. So, to my father's way of thinking, my passion was for something with an artistic bent even though it was photography and film-making as opposed to painting. He'd have been far happier if I'd wanted to go back to running sheep stations if I was determined to turn my back on banking, law or all those pursuits—chosen something that would help run the Moore empire at least, rather than the dubious world of art.'

'So you took your art somewhere dangerous?'

He eyed her quizzically. 'I rather think that was a motive, but I was only twenty-three and still capable of being riled by him.'

'Only twenty-three when you first started making wildlife documentaries?'

He nodded. 'All the same, it was a motive beneath a motive, for I had always been fascinated by big game. But, of course, once I got to Africa with that slightly do or die, blast you, Dad attitude—and five boring years of law school under my belt—things changed. It got into my blood. There's something else that—' He stopped.

'Please tell me,' she said quietly.

He studied her for a long moment, his blue eyes narrowed and a little bleak. 'There's something about fortunes and family dynasties that's stultifying and claustrophobic. It's an awfully insular way of life because the name and the fortune come to mean more than anything else. For example, what my father was most concerned about was that Gareth and I would be able to take over from him eventually. That's—' he paused and shrugged '—what prompted me to do it all without a cent of his money.'

'You mean you started from scratch?' Her eyes widened. 'But how?'

'I was articled to a law firm while I was doing my degree so I earned a bit and in my spare time I did social photography—wedding albums and videos, twenty-first birthdays and so on.' He looked rueful.

Louise sat back and only then became aware of how she'd been sitting forward absolutely intently. 'Do you still resent your father?'

'No.' He smiled faintly. 'But then fate or whatever has been kind to me. As for my father, well, two things have worked in my favour recently. He does not approve of Roslyn White and considers that I may, for once, have had more sense than Gareth.'

'I see. What's the other thing?'

'He's taken to introducing me as his famous son.'

Louise smiled. 'The return of the prodigal,' she murmured.

'I'm quite sure that when the dust dies down around Gareth we'll be back to normal.'

'That sounds a bit cynical. Maybe he's mellowing with age, your father?'

Richard was silent for a time. Then he stirred and said wryly, 'He's also starting to talk about how it's time I got this wanderlust out of my system and settled down.'

'Oh, no!'

'You don't have to look so shocked,' he said amusedly. 'It doesn't mean a thing to me.'

'It wasn't that, it was, well—' She broke off and grimaced.

'It was what?' His blue eyes probed hers until some
colour stole into her cheeks.

'I...I just thought that *me* on top of your father, well,
particularly with someone as allergic— Oh, damn,' she
said helplessly. 'Forget it.' But she had second thoughts
immediately. 'Perhaps I couldn't have come at a worse
time is what I'm trying to say, but it sounds—unreal and
silly put like that.'

He considered and his lips twitched. 'Not if you seriously believe I'm still negatively influenced by my father.'

'Are you—sure? That you aren't?' she asked hesi-
tantly.

'Louise—' he looked even more amused '—yes. Are
you sure you're still not considering me as a likely can-
didate for your famed benevolence?'

She looked away and grew redder. 'Do I really come
across as such a—do-gooder?'

'Sometimes. Not in bed, though.'

'That's—'

'Not fair, Richard,' he mocked gently, and stood up.
'Talking of which, I think it's time we turned in. Happy
to go home tomorrow, by the way?'

She sat very still in her chair, watching him. He'd
changed for dinner into his new jeans and blue and green
checked shirt and he looked tall and terrifyingly attractive as he put their cups away. She wondered suddenly
what he'd been like as a twenty-three-year-old rebel with

the courage and the insight to turn his back on family tradition, a fortune and a dynasty. Was it any wonder he was a loner?

'Louise?'

She blinked and realized he'd come to stand in front of her with a query in his eyes. She swallowed and tried to resist the impulse claiming her. I'll regret this, she thought, but then I'll always regret Richard Moore and at least I could do it on *my* terms... Is that what I mean, or that I could do it proudly and honestly and *remember* it in those terms? Instead of the horror and confusion that overwhelmed me last time?

She swallowed again, stood up carefully—and told him what was going through her mind. And once again had the doubtful felicity of arresting him completely.

'Louise,' he said at last, with a little flare of shock still in his eyes, 'that would not—'

'Change anything?' she said very quietly. 'I know; I'm not trying to change anything.'

'That wasn't what I was going to say.'

'It doesn't matter what you were going to say.' Her voice was quiet and firm, her eyes steady. 'What matters is whether you believe in me at all. Whether you believe I have the courage to know that I can't change you, the courage to want to end this in a way that will give me some peace and restore some self-esteem.'

'There was *never* any need for a lack of self-esteem,' he said intently.

A faint smile curved her lips. 'Perhaps you don't know women as well as you think, Richard Moore. Or perhaps I'm different.' She lifted her slim shoulders. 'Whatever, I do admire and respect you very much, but I take full responsibility for knowing what I need better than you do at the moment. I'll let you go, I promise, with no hard feelings.'

He swore beneath his breath. 'Look, what I was going to say was—we were lucky last time, but only...two fools would imagine we could keep on being lucky.'

'It's too soon,' she said simply.

'How on earth can you know?'

'I know my cycle because it runs like clockwork. If I didn't believe I was safe, I wouldn't be doing this.' For a moment, Louise Brown, schoolmistress, showed in her eyes and the way she held her chin, and then she did something she'd longed to do for days.

She moved into his arms and laid her forehead on his shoulder to add with a husky little tremor in her voice, 'I don't know how *well* I can do it with a broken wrist, so don't expect too much, but—if you could just hold me, Richard, I would love nothing better than to find a way to make love to you now.'

'My dear...' He stopped and his arms came up around her, then he swore again.

But she raised her mouth to his and said, 'Shh...' against his lips, then kissed him.

CHAPTER EIGHT

'LOUISE BROWN,' he said softly.

'You never call me Lou. My friends do,' she whispered. There was only one lamp on and they were naked beneath the duvet. They were lying in each other's arms and he was running his hand through the luxurious disorder of her hair.

'I like Louise. It's old-fashioned and pretty. How's your wrist?'

'So far so good—this seems to be a good spot for it.' 'This' was lying across Richard's waist out of harm's way.

'Not quite the fireworks of last time but just as nice in its own way.' He smiled into her eyes and she went weak with longing. 'We're talking this time.'

'It was—lovely.'

He drew his hand from her hair and slid it down her back to cup the curve of her hip, then he guided her leg over his. 'So much so I have to do it again. Do you mind?'

'How could I mind?' She moved closer so that the tips of her breasts brushed the wall of his chest, at the same time as she kissed the strong column of his throat and the tanned skin of his shoulder. She said, 'I'm overflowing with desire myself. Strange what you can do with a broken wrist!' She lifted her green gaze to his and smiled back, then stilled as he moved her away slightly and touched her nipples at the same time as his hand on her hip moved to explore more and more intimately with the lightest touch.

She made a slight sound of sheer pleasure and tipped her head back, closing her eyes as her body thrummed like a taut bow, and his lips replaced his fingers on her nipples.

'Richard,' she murmured. 'Oh, Richard—I'm dying—that's too nice.'

'It's almost unbearable for me,' he responded, and repositioned her so that he could enter her with a strong thrust, and that lovely rhythm started to claim them both.

Their breathing quickened and she arched herself against him as he held her hard, hip to hip, with both hands now, and they climaxed together with an intensity that left her shuddering in his arms with such rapture, she was bereft of speech.

And it seemed he could find no words for an age as the splendour of their lovemaking subsided slowly and his arms loosened to cradle her slim, spent body to him with heart-breaking gentleness.

Only then did he say into her hair, 'I was wrong. About the fireworks, I mean. OK?'

Louise lifted her face at last and tried to smile. 'You were right about one thing—a Taj Mahal seems paltry by comparison.'

'Don't knock a Taj Mahal. If I could build one to you now, I would.' He traced her mouth, then kissed it softly. 'Go to sleep, Miss Brown.'

'Don't remind me—this must be my alter ego.'

'This—all this exquisiteness?'

Her breath caught in her throat. 'I think you're—superb, incidentally.'

He laughed quietly, kissed the tip of her nose, and presently she fell asleep peacefully.

It took Richard longer to sleep, though. After he'd switched the lamp off he lay for some time considering this latest development, with no trace of a smile now.

How on earth am I going to walk away from her? he wondered. Not least because I don't want to. But...how the hell could it work? She won't settle for anything less than all or nothing. If I believe in *nothing* else, I believe that. *Why* the hell am I like this? She couldn't be less like Ros if she tried. Except—his lips twisted, then he closed his eyes abruptly—she can be so stubborn, and sure she's right and holier-than-thou...

It was nearly an hour later before he fell asleep with no solution in mind.

'We need to talk,' he said as he drove her car down Mount Tamborine.

It was a wet, muggy morning and they both slept through breakfast, and later found themselves in a rush to vacate their rooms on time.

'Don't.' She put her hand briefly over his on the gear lever. 'It's all been said.'

'No, it hasn't,' he replied tersely. 'If you imagine I can just walk away from you, Louise, you're not as sane as I thought.'

She glanced at him to see his mouth set in a hard line and said with a little sigh, 'You're going to spoil it all for me, Richard, aren't you?'

'What the hell does that mean?'

'I told you, last night.'

'That was before—amongst other things—I helped

you to shower and dress this morning, even brushed your hair for you.'

Louise bit her lip as she remembered the warmth and intimacy of him soaping her body for her, then drying her carefully despite their rush. But she knew what she had to do, although she swallowed several times and prayed that she sounded calmer than she felt.

'Look,' she said quietly, 'it could never work. I think we both know that. I'm too...whatever you like to call it—'

'Dogmatic?' he supplied dryly.

She flinched inwardly but managed to say coolly, 'If you like. And you're too independent.'

'That doesn't mean to say we have to cut every single tie.'

'What do you suggest? That we have a reunion twice a year or something like that?' She looked at him levelly.

He swore softly.

'Richard, go—please,' she said with a catch in her voice but that same steady look. 'I know what would happen if I tried to change things and I know myself well enough to know I *would* try to change things. It could only end in disaster. Whereas now—' she blinked and sniffed, then smiled at him '—I at least have you as a shining knight in my heart, however unreal it may be, and you, I hope, will have the knowledge that I could never regret that it happened.'

'Do you seriously mean that?' He frowned at the road.

'Yes.'

'So,' he said slowly, 'you propose to go on with your life just as before?'

'Not quite. Either Neil will move or I will—that's something we'll have to work out. But I wouldn't leave

MacRae Place. And I'll go on teaching. And sailing and playing the piano. You don't have to worry about me,' she assured him.

He was silent for a long time and his thoughts would have taken Louise by surprise had she been able to read them. Because the truth was Richard Moore was battling with several strong emotions. One of which, he told himself ruefully, was a distinctly dog-in-the-manger reaction. Back on the back burner, he mused. So passionate one moment, then detached and more of an enigma than you ever were, my beautiful Louise Brown. How do you do it? Do you have *any* idea that I feel somewhat deflated to think of you going on serenely just as before?

'Richard?'

He glanced at her but that was a mistake because he knew he'd carry a mental picture of her as she sat beside him, with her gorgeous ash-blonde hair loose and curly, her calm green eyes with their little golden flecks, with those severe lips that could soften so deliciously that were now quite steady—he would carry that image with him for a long, long time.

It crossed his mind to wonder whether any man would completely fuse the two Louise Browns—the practical, sane, sensible, compulsive one and the girl who dreamt of Shah Jahan and Mumtaz Mahal—into one completely loving woman? Obviously it's not me, he thought dryly, then moved restlessly at the awful irony of the thought.

'May I write to you?' he said at last.

'If you like, although I may not answer.'

And that was how they left it.

Once they got home to MacRae Place, Neil and Eve were there to greet them and it was plain that they were dying of curiosity. But for once Eve forbore to put her thoughts into words. In fact, Louise thought she detected a slightly subdued air about the other girl although her brown eyes were so clearly speculative.

Don't tell me Neil went ahead and told her, Louise mused exasperatedly.

But, if anything, the possibility of this helped her to put on a masterly performance as Richard explained he was leaving that afternoon.

Friendly, affectionate even, but quite unperturbed was the air she projected as she offered to drive him to the airport, then looked rueful as she remembered her wrist.

But Richard had other ideas. He refused Neil's offer to do the same, saying he'd rather get a taxi from the hotel; but he did spend a few minutes with Neil in his study before he left for the Mirage. What was said, Louise had no idea, but Neil emerged looking slightly reassured.

And all that was left was to say goodbye to him at the garden gate.

'If—' he stood looking down at her with those blue, blue eyes '—anything goes wrong with your timing, Neil knows how to get in touch with me.'

'You didn't—?' Louise hesitated.

'No, I didn't tell him. But I'm telling you that the best laid plans in that direction have been known to go awry—and I have the right to know.'

She swallowed. 'Of course. But they won't.'

He smiled slightly. 'Stubborn to the end.'

She drew a breath. 'How many times have I told you that?'

This time his smile was wry but genuine and he bent his head to kiss her lightly on the brow. 'Goodbye, my lovely Louise Brown. If there is one thing I wish for you, it's that your Shah Jahan comes along.'

It was rather strange, she thought, how calm she felt, yet she had to acknowledge that there was something slightly eerie about it. As if time were standing still when in fact it was ticking away inexorably. Very soon this big man who could be so scathing but also so nice would be gone for good. It was as if the air around them had gone still and the delicate perfume of the camellias, the scent of grass, the hum of traffic beyond the wall, the blue sky above would always be imprinted on her heart, encapsulated in a moment of time for her, for ever.

But she said serenely, 'Goodbye, Richard. Your taxi's here. Look after yourself and I very much hope the same for you—that your Muntaz will arrive too.' She smiled up at him and turned to walk away without a backward glance, although no one would ever know the effort it cost her.

She held on to her composure long enough to go back inside to face Neil and Eve, with no inkling of the surprise that lay in store for her...

CHAPTER NINE

TWELVE months later Louise was sitting in the garden reviewing the year.

She'd tried desperately not to let the significance of this date prey on her mind but in the end the power of her memories had been too great a force to resist. She sat beneath the canvas awning with a blue sky beyond and camellias once again in bloom above the pretty little statue of a naked lady on the grass.

It was twelve months to the day since she'd last seen Richard Moore, since she'd sent him away, secure in her conviction that she was doing the right thing, and not knowing that the next few months would be a living torment. That she wouldn't be able to get him out of her heart or mind, that she would physically ache to be in his arms and that nothing she did would help.

Months when her beloved MacRae Place, the beach and the *Georgia 2* had been an unbearable reminder of him and she'd thought at times that she would never recover. Thought wildly of going away, anywhere, to be rid of the memories and the sense of loss, as well as the awful fear that what she'd done was quite wrong...

On top of this there'd been the trauma of trying to hide it all from Neil. Although that, as it happened, had been more a matter of pride...

Neil and Eve had married—she smiled as she thought of it.

The Parkers had insisted on a huge, elaborate wedding

for their only daughter, and Eve's sheer happiness had made her a lovely bride. Although Louise had offered to sell her share of the town house to them, Eve had decided she'd ratter start from scratch and she and Neil had bought an apartment close by. Louise had, however, sold her share of the *Georgia 2* to Eve.

She closed her eyes and lay back. Beyond the high wall she could hear MacRae Place going about its business and her thoughts panned slowly down the months...

He had written. Letters that had sometimes taken weeks to reach her, posted from exotic places that were obviously unreliable, postage-wise. Letters that she had never replied to but cherished all the same. Letters that had told her little except that he was still doing what he loved best; but he'd made her laugh to his descriptions and enabled her to feel as if she could breathe the scents and sounds of those far-away places.

To counteract all sorts of things, she'd decided to give piano lessons in her spare time and now, literally, had so little spare time she even felt guilty about sitting in the garden as she was. But it had helped to be so busy. The power of the memories had eased gradually although, when she was tired and alone, they still had the ability to sneak up on her and cause her to catch her breath with sheer, sharp pain. Like today, she thought, then moved with relief at a little sound.

She stood up and bent over the pram beside her. 'So you're awake, sweetheart,' she crooned, and picked up the three-month-old little girl who was so amazingly like her. 'I thought you were going to sleep right through lunchtime! I—'

She stopped and straightened as the gate in the wall clicked open and her lips parted incredulously. Because

Richard Moore stood there and it was almost as if he'd never left. Khaki shirt, patched jeans, dusty boots and his hair roughly cut, blue shadows on his jaw...

I'm dreaming, Louise thought, and blinked frantically. She must also have clutched the baby too tight because it made a squeak of protest.

And Richard his face pale, his blue eyes unbelievably hard, walked forward at last until he was right beside her. He looked down at the little girl in her arms with her down of ash-blonde hair and the unmistakable resemblance.

'You *fool*,' he said through his teeth, and there was an almost murderous glint in his eyes as they clashed with hers. 'I didn't believe even you could be so blindly stubborn, Louise Brown, or so completely unable to ever admit you could be *wrong* about anything. How long did you plan to keep this a secret from me? For ever?'

For some reason Louise's tongue seemed to want to cleave to the roof of her mouth. 'I...didn't...I...that is,' she stammered as his gaze seemed to scorch her, then sheer angry disbelief came to her rescue 'What are you doing here?'

'What do you think?' he returned insolently, scanning her from top to toe. She was wearing a loose, comfortable cotton smock with yellow dots on a pale grey background and her hair was tied back with a yellow ribbon. She wore no make-up and, perhaps even more significantly, it was a weekday.

'I have no idea...' she started to say.

He laughed harshly. 'Don't you? But before we get onto that—what happened to those highly moral, holier-than-thou sentiments you expressed on the subject of little girls—' he glanced expressively at the baby's pink attire '—growing up without a constant father figure in their lives?'

Louise was as pale as he was now. 'I still stand by them,' she said tautly. 'This…'

'Or did you, in your inimitable way of believing you have *all* the answers, decide *you* could be the one to change the system? Be the one who could be both father and mother to a child?'

'How dare you?' Louise whispered. 'If you came here for the express purpose of insulting me you can turn around and just go away again.'

'I didn't, as it happens,' he replied roughly. 'I came to tell you I can't live without you and I've arranged my life accordingly—'

'Is that so?' Louise marvelled. 'In spite of your conviction that I'm so inimitably pigheaded and superior? I do hope you haven't made too many new arrangements for your life, Richard, because it will have been a waste of time so far as *I'm* concerned.'

He opened his mouth to reply but the baby chose to make its presence felt. Its rosebud mouth quivered and a reproachful little cry issued. Richard blinked twice and said slowly and in a different voice, 'What did you call her?'

'Millicent—but we call her Milly.' She repositioned the baby in her arms and kissed the downy head.

'We? So Neil… Well, he's obviously gone along with this deception. How did you persuade him to do that? I told him how to get in touch with me express—if ever you needed me.'

'That *was* kind of you. I suppose that's what you two were discussing in his study the day you left? You told me—' her eyes were green and stormy '—you *hadn't*—'

'I didn't. Go into details,' he said with a shrug. 'But—'

'Then you thought I might go into a decline of some kind,' she taunted. 'You were wrong, Richard. I didn't need you then and I don't need you now so—'

'Here I am! Late as usual!'

It was Eve's voice, panting a little as she dashed through the garden gate. 'Sorry, Lou, but I got held up. Hope she hasn't been screaming for a feed— Glory be! If it isn't Richard Moore!'

'None other,' Louise agreed dryly. 'And no, she hasn't been screaming for a feed, but it won't be long before she's a little desperate. Will it, Milly, darling? Never mind, your mum's here.' She kissed the baby again, handed her over to Eve, stared deliberately into Richard's stunned eyes for a moment, then swung on her heel and walked out of the garden through the gate.

'I wondered if I'd find you here.'

Louise looked up briefly but said nothing. She was sitting on top of a dune, watching the sea, so blue today with a breeze rippling its surface.

Richard sat down beside her. 'Can I say in my defence that a lot of it was wishful thinking?'

'You can *say* what you like.'

He studied her profile. It was austere, although the sun had brought a flush to her cheeks, some beads of perspiration to her neck and little tendrils of hair were escaping her ribbons. 'The baby does look a lot like you.'

'She's my niece.'

He was silent for a time, then he said, 'I'm no expert on babies but she'd be just about the right age, wouldn't she?'

'Look, Richard, if you're trying to get me to admit it was a mistake anyone might have made—'

'Not anyone,' he said quietly. 'And not something even I should have assumed, but—it is also a weekday and mid-term, I should imagine.'

'Exactly. A mid-term holiday to be precise, which is why I offered to baby-sit for Eve.'

'I'm sorry. I—' he paused with his hands clasped on his bent knees '—I had planned a different reconciliation on this—particular day.'

'You surprise me.'

'Could I—start again?'

Louise made a frustrated sound. 'What would be the point? You—'

'Got off on the wrong foot— Look, I've apologized and tried to explain.'

'But don't you see,' she said evenly, 'how the truth can pop out under those circumstances? So if you've come to tell me you've wrested yourself away from a life you love for—I don't know—reasons of guilt or whatever—'

'It's not that.'

'It has to be something like that!' She turned to him at last, angrily and incredulously. 'Why else would you do it if, in your heart of hearts, you believe I'm a stubborn, superior know-all?'

'Would you at least let me tell you what I've done? And why?'

She gestured futilely and looked away.

'It—came to me,' he said slowly, 'that I was clinging on to a crusade that had run its course.'

'I don't suppose the elephant or the rhino would see it that way,' she observed curtly.

He smiled faintly, then sobered immediately. 'I was talking about my own personal crusade. The one to do with shaking off the shackles of my father and the Moore empire. It came to me that I no longer had to go away to resist being sucked into the family machine, nor did I have to go away to do what I really love best—and that's to make films.'

'You said Africa was in your blood,' she whispered.

He grinned. 'I thought it was. I now know that the only thing in my blood is you. If I can't have you, Louise, Africa and everything to do with it is no substitute.'

'If this is all true—*if*—'

'I know what you're going to say,' he broke in. 'It took me a long time to work it out? In fact the disaffection started to creep in before I even got back. But I'd signed two contracts which I had to honour and I knew I couldn't come back to you unless I had something concrete to offer.'

'And what would you have done if I'd upped and married someone in the interim, Richard?'

He hesitated. 'That was something Neil swore he would keep me posted on.'

Louise gasped. 'I don't believe it!'

'My dear,' he said somewhat dryly, 'you were the one who insisted I go.'

'I...I...all the same...'

'You were the one,' he continued inexorably, 'who said goodbye to me with not the least sign of regret. Who appeared to have everything in such control, who had created a neat compartment, if you like, for what had happened between us where it could lie in the realms of fantasy and gather dust—just one of those things,' he said brutally.

'I didn't—' She broke off abruptly and swallowed. 'What did you tell Neil?' she asked hastily.

'That I didn't know if I was what you were looking for but I'd like the chance to—try again one day.'

'He n-never said a word.' Her voice shook. 'Mind you, I—' She swallowed again. 'And then there was the irony of *Eve* being pregnant.'

'So you didn't have to go through any charade to convince Neil to go ahead and marry her?'

'No,' Louise said after an age. 'All the same, I did.'

'And was it a charade, Louise?' His voice was quiet and steady and his eyes seemed to be looking into her soul.

She looked away, then stood up restlessly, brushing sand from her dress.

'Louise?' He got up in one swift, lithe movement and took her hand.

She tried to pull away and, when she couldn't, closed her eyes briefly, then squared her shoulders. 'Yes. I ached and yearned for you, Richard. I couldn't believe—I mean, it hit me like a train once you'd gone—and I'd done it all by my own hand. And I've wondered and been tormented ever since because life without you was so wrong, when I'd been so sure I was doing the right thing. But—'

'My darling Louise—you don't know what it means to me to hear you say that.'

'But, Richard, no, please…'

He'd released her hand to take her in his arms but she put her hands up beseechingly, and she stepped back.

'You are right about me in some respects.' Her green eyes were tortured.

'And you were right about me in a lot of respects. I thought I was cut out to be a loner. I *didn't* see how we could bridge all the differences and the gaps. Now I know that my life would be one long void without you. Can I—' he paused and reached for her hand again '—say that part of my hostility and disbelief when I saw you with that baby was to do with a bitter feeling of being shut out? *Our* child, I thought, but you'd chosen to go through it all alone when I would have so much wanted to be with you.'

Louise stared at him. 'If only you knew—' She broke off and bit her lip.

'Say it.'

She looked down, sighed, then said barely audibly, 'How many times I've wished she was our child.'

This time she didn't resist when he took her in his arms so strongly that for a moment she couldn't breathe.

'We need to get away from here,' he said ruefully, some minutes later.

'Oh!' Louise came to earth and looked around to find that they were the object of some interest and amusement. Her cheeks reddened as one young surfer whistled at them. Then her embarrassment became consternation. 'Eve! I was going to look after Milly again this afternoon!'

He smiled down into her eyes. 'Eve said not to worry about it. She's taken Miss Milly home.'

'How did she…?'

'Know this might be on the cards? I told her that, come hell or high water, this time I was never going to let you go.'

Louise relaxed against him but almost immediately looked concerned again. 'Richard, I knew it would—be so foolish to want to change you or— I'm worried about this,' she confessed.

He said wryly, 'Will you come somewhere a little less public so that I can reassure you?'

'Of course. We could go home—'

'I had in mind my room at the Sheraton. My things are there; I dropped them off and came straight over. Not that I thought you'd be at home but I was hoping to catch Neil.'

'All right, but—' She stopped.

'I'll have to explain myself fully before I can hope for any more intimacies?' His lips quirked.

Louise sighed. 'I may often sound like a schoolmarm. Don't say I didn't warn you.'

He laughed and kissed her lightly. 'Let's go.'

His room was vast with a view of the ocean, cool tiled floors, louvres at the windows and an attractive decor. His two battered bags stood in the middle of the floor, not even opened, let alone unpacked.

'Would you mind if I had a shower? Why don't you order us some lunch?' he suggested as she stood in the middle of the room looking pale and oddly apprehensive.

'What would you like?'

'Anything—you choose.' He handed her the room-service menu, and went away to the bathroom.

Why do I feel like this? Louise wondered. How do I feel? As if I can't believe it's true? She stared into space for a moment, swallowed and sat down on the bed to ring for lunch.

It came quickly, a choice of cold meat and salads,

beautifully presented, and with a complimentary bottle
of wine in a frosted silver cooler.

Richard emerged from the bathroom at the same time,
showered, shaved, in a T-shirt and shorts, drying his hair
on a towel. He dealt swiftly with the waiter and they
were alone.

'Sit down,' he said gently, pulling out a chair for her.
'This is where we began, almost,' he added whimsically
as he poured some golden Riesling into her glass. 'With
cold meat and salad.' He smiled down at her and her
poor, battered heart started to beat heavily. He put the
glass in her hand. 'Drink some.'

She did and felt some colour come back to her cheeks.

He sat down opposite and, without consulting her,
dished up for them both. 'I could kick myself,' he said
quietly. 'I've done nothing but...trample about like a
herd of elephants ever since I laid eyes on you.'

'I'm OK,' Louise said huskily. 'It's just, well, shock,
I guess.'

'Have some lunch,' he suggested, and when she
started to eat he said, 'You have changed me, Louise,
but it's not something I'll ever regret.'

'That's easy to say now, Richard, but...ten years on
it might be different.'

'No,' he contradicted her. 'Because if, ten years on, I
was still doing what I've been doing I would be the
worse for it. That's not to say I'll suddenly lose interest
in wildlife and conservation—I never will—but I need
to broaden my horizons now. My medium is film and
there are endless avenues I want to explore through it.
I'm going into mainstream directing. You could say I've
served my apprenticeship. I'd like to think I've served

the planet in some small way—' he shrugged ruefully '—but now's the time to move on.'

She couldn't tear her gaze from his.

'And, yes, you were the catalyst that brought this about, Louise,' he went on, 'only it doesn't stop there. After Ros, there seemed to be another reason to stay away and I persuaded myself that I was better off alone. Now I know I was only burying my head in the sand, taking the easy option and—' he paused and looked at her very directly '—investing all women with the grasping, ambitious, designing machinations of one of you.

'The truth is, though, that I can't even remember her face now. She has no substance; she's gone where she belongs—where I should have consigned her immediately. Out of my heart. There is now not only no regret but no sense of bitterness or sense of betrayal. She's gone.'

Louise found she couldn't speak.

He put his hand over hers. 'And if,' he continued barely audibly, 'you should decide I'm—not your Shah Jahan I still would go forward, Louise.'

'Richard.' Her eyes were misted with tears, and she tried to speak, smiled shakily and tried again. 'I love you…'

'Third time lucky.'

Richard raised his head and looked down at her. 'Did you say what I think you said?'

Louise smiled, a little embarrassed. 'It just popped out.'

'I agree with the lucky bit—' he smoothed the tangle of her hair '—but that's not quite accurate. It's the fourth time we've made love.'

This fourth time had eclipsed their previous lovemaking as a mutual hunger had overwhelmed them in a bitter-sweet reunion that had left them clinging to each other as if on a distant shore in uncharted waters, so powerfully emotional and physical had it been.

'Well—yes, you're right, of course, but—'

'I know I'm right,' he teased. 'I have the very clearest recollection of each and every moment of each and every time.'

'Do you?' Her expression was fascinated. 'Well, so do I,' she murmured hastily, 'but what I meant—'

'I should hope so,' he said gravely, 'considering what a nightmare those recollections have made of my life for the past twelve months, Miss Brown.'

'Will you let me finish, Mr Moore?'

'Be my guest.'

She mistrusted the wicked glint in his eyes devoutly but she said, 'I meant this is our third *encounter* and— you know very well what I meant!'

'I just like to be correct on all details,' he replied innocently. 'Because I always knew how easily distracted you could be.'

She laughed softly, then sobered suddenly.

'Don't.' He stroked her cheek and gathered her close. 'It's over now, all the pain and confusion, my darling. We've come to an upland of love and joy. When will you marry me?'

'That's lovely,' she whispered, and slid her hands around his neck. 'Whenever you like. Tell me some more about your plans.'

So they lay together in the vast bed and she learnt about the Australian movie he'd been asked to direct later in the year and they made plans for their wedding.

'I had this thought for a honeymoon—Africa.'

Her eyes widened. 'But…'

'I know—don't worry, I won't be tempted. But there are some things I need to share with you, a part of my life that we can see together, then close together. The Victoria Falls, Serengeti and the Masai Mara, Ngorongoro. Kilimanjaro and Kruger. The Mountains of the Moon.'

Her happiness shone in her eyes, so much so that he was visibly affected and any doubts he'd had about being the one to transform her into a completely loving woman were swept away.

And presently he said, 'We never could keep our hands off each other, my dearest love, and nothing's changed. Do you mind?'

'Mind? I love it,' she said softly. 'So that accounts for it?'

'That, plus something we were both sceptical about. It is how people fall in love, sometimes, don't you agree? Out of the blue, just like the thunder and lightning that first night on the boat.'

She said softly, 'I do.'

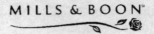

MILLS & BOON

Next Month's Romances

Each month you can choose from a wide variety of romance novels from Mills & Boon®. Below are the new titles to look out for next month from the Presents™ and Enchanted™ series.

Presents™

MARRIAGE MAKE UP	Penny Jordan
THE MILLIONAIRE'S MISTRESS	Miranda Lee
THE RIGHT FIANCÉ?	Lee Wilkinson
MARRIAGE AT A DISTANCE	Sara Craven
EXPECTANT MISTRESS	Sara Wood
WIFE FOR A DAY	Kate Walker
AN INNOCENT AFFAIR	Kim Lawrence
NOT WITHOUT A WIFE!	Alexandra Sellers

Enchanted™

AGENDA: ATTRACTION!	Jessica Steele
UNDERCOVER HUSBAND	Rebecca Winters
A GROOM FOR GWEN	Jeanne Allan
GENTLEMEN PREFER...BRUNETTES	Liz Fielding
HIS UNEXPECTED FAMILY	Grace Green
READY-MADE BRIDE	Janelle Denison
SHEIK DADDY	Barbara McMahon
HER VERY OWN HUSBAND	Lauryn Chandler

On sale from 10th August 1998

H1 9807

Available at most branches of
WH Smith, John Menzies, Martins, Tesco,
Asda, Volume One, Sainsbury and Safeway

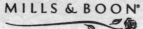

RONA JAFFE

Five Women

Once a week, five women meet over dinner and
drinks at the Yellowbird, their favourite
Manhattan bar. To the shared table they bring
their troubled pasts; their hidden secrets.
And through their friendship, each will find
a courageous new beginning.

Five Women is an *"insightful look at female
relationships."*

—Publishers Weekly

1-55166-424-0
AVAILABLE IN PAPERBACK
FROM AUGUST, 1998

DEBBIE MACOMBER

Married in Montana

Needing a safe place for her sons to grow up, Molly
Cogan decided it was time to return home.
Home to Sweetgrass Montana.
Home to her grandfather's ranch.

*"Debbie Macomber's name on a book is a guarantee
of delightful, warm-hearted romance."*
—Jayne Ann Krentz

1-55166-400-3
**AVAILABLE IN PAPERBACK
FROM AUGUST, 1998**

4 FREE
books and a surprise gift!

We would like to take this opportunity to thank you for reading this Mills & Boon® book by offering you the chance to take FOUR more specially selected titles from the Presents™ series absolutely FREE! We're also making this offer to introduce you to the benefits of the Reader Service™—

- ★ FREE home delivery
- ★ FREE gifts and competitions
- ★ FREE monthly newsletter
- ★ Books available before they're in the shops
- ★ Exclusive Reader Service discounts

Accepting these FREE books and gift places you under no obligation to buy, you may cancel at any time, even after receiving your free shipment. Simply complete your details below and return the entire page to the address below. *You don't even need a stamp!*

YES! Please send me 4 free Presents books and a surprise gift. I understand that unless you hear from me, I will receive 6 superb new titles every month for just £2.30 each, postage and packing free. I am under no obligation to purchase any books and may cancel my subscription at any time. The free books and gift will be mine to keep in any case.

P8YE

Ms/Mrs/Miss/Mr.................................Initials ....
BLOCK CAPITALS PLEASE

Surname ....

Address ....

....

....Postcode................................

Send this whole page to:
THE READER SERVICE, FREEPOST, CROYDON, CR9 3WZ
(Eire readers please send coupon to: P.O. BOX 4546, DUBLIN 24.)

Mills & Boon Presents is being used as a trademark.

The Sunday Times **bestselling author**

PENNY JORDAN

TO LOVE, HONOUR &

Motherhood, marriage, obsession, betrayal and family duty... the latest blockbuster from Penny Jordan has it all. Claudia and Garth's marriage is in real trouble when they adopt a baby and Garth realises that the infant is his!

"Women everywhere will find pieces of themselves in Jordan's characters."

—Publishers Weekly

MIRA®

1-55166-396-1
AVAILABLE FROM JULY 1998